DISCARD

MICK LIUBINSKAS

CORAL GABLES

She's Building a Robot: A STEM Novel

Library of Congress Cataloging-in-Publication number: 2020940957
ISBN: (print) 978-1-64250-341-8
BISAC: JUV014000—JUVENILE FICTION/ Girls & Women

Printed in the United States of America

T-Minus Twenty-One

The first time I was expelled, it wasn't my fault. Not entirely. It was caused by a hundred seemingly small moments. Any one of them could have gone differently. But they didn't.

The moment that started it all off was an increasingly noisy Friday afternoon in Computer Science.

"Ok, fine, books away, let's do a challenge," said Mrs. D'Silva. "Here's a logic puzzle. If anyone can solve it, the lesson is over."

"Well, you mere mortals just leave it to the genius," said Dalk.

I looked at Dalk and my mouth dried up. I'd known Dalk for years now and had never once directly spoken to him. He was popular, smart, and he seemed to be able to do whatever he wanted. It's unfair. I shook the thought away and turned back to the board.

I like puzzles. I always have. The thrill and the frustration. That was "Home AZ," though, not "School AZ." They were two very different people and I took great care to keep them separate. School AZ didn't win challenges like this.

Mrs. D'Silva wrote on the board:

Three identical robots are sitting in a row. Ayanna Howard, a roboticist, wanted to work out which robot was which. What she knows is that ENIAC always tells the truth, Bender always lies, and R2D2 sometimes tells the truth and sometimes lies.

Ayanna asked the first robot, "Which robot is in the middle of you three?"

The answer she received was, "That is ENIAC."

Ayanna then asked the robot in the middle, "What is your name?"

The response given was, "I'm R2D2."

Ayanna turned to the robot on the right, then asked, "Who is that in the middle?"

The robot replied, "That is Bender."

Ayanna asked the same question three times and received three different answers.

Who was who?

I started to write down a few ideas. I could work this out. But I couldn't win. People like Dalk win. It was unfair, but that's just the way things were. This was just one challenge.

Over my stomach sliding and my mind flipping, a thought surfaced. As I turned to the board to look at the puzzle, I thought of my mother who loves puzzles. Her voice floated into my head saying, "AZ, what is the whole puzzle about? Don't just start. Start right."

Read the puzzle. Think. Read the puzzle. Think. Read the puzzle.

"Don't fret, my people," said Dalk. "Everyone will be cheering my name. Just like every time I win our robot-building competition."

A few of my classmates were looking out the windows. I leaned into the paper on my desk. Thoughts bounced against questions and suddenly I had the answer. But, as usual, I wasn't going to say anything. I was going to keep it to myself.

Then, from some far-flung corner of the universe, a new sensation entered my stomach and made itself at home. It was bold and felt good, but also scary. I straightened my back and lifted my head.

"First is R2D2, second is Bender, third is ENIAC," I said loudly and clearly.

Silence. Then someone gasped.

What just happened? Did I really just do that?

"What? No way," Dalk said. "I don't think that's—"

"She's right," interrupted Mrs. D'Silva, smiling.

"Oh, come on. *Aye Zed* beat me? I've never lost a challenge. Did you give her the answers or something?" Dalk said.

Mrs. D'Silva stopped smiling as she walked down the aisle to Dalk. "I beg your pardon? Watch how you speak to me, young man. I don't care whose son you are. I certainly did *not* give her the answer. And it's pronounced Aye Zee, not Aye Zed," She looked down at Dalk's work. "She got it right before you and that's all there is to it."

Dalk scowled at Mrs. D'Silva and me in turn.

I looked around and saw people's expressions shifting between smiling at her and sneaking a worried peek at Dalk.

With his face turning red, Dalk knocked his chair over and walked out the room.

"I was wondering when you were going to turn up," said Mrs. D'Silva, smiling at me again.

Looking around the room and feeling the sweat roll down my forehead, I wondered whether I'd just slapped a "social pie" into my own face.

T-Minus Twenty

Just one hour later, I was in the school principal's office facing the consequences.

Jax, the billionaire CEO of Jax Robotics, benefactor of 99 percent of our school's fundraising, and the father of Dalk, was pacing the very small room in very small steps.

"I want her expelled! I want her fired! I want you to give a public apology to my son. I want it today!" yelled Jax, spittle flying.

What had I done?

"Ok. Ok. Ok. Please calm down," said Principal Tajek. His hands attempted to smooth over the tension of this strange group, squeezed into his beige office. Around the room was Mrs. D'Silva, Jax, Dalk, and my dad, wishing he were somewhere else. The room smelled like everyone had their shoes off while eating super-strong mints.

"Impossible. I cannot 'calm down.' My son's honor, my family's honor, *my* honor has been torn to shreds by some unqualified hack and a clear cheater," Jax yelled, slamming both fists on the table three times, knocking over a plastic cup full of chewed pens.

"Your son made an unfounded accusation and his behavior was completely inappropriate," Mrs. D'Silva said, arms folded. "And quite frankly, it's about the one-hundredth time and if he wasn't…"

"Impossible. My son would never act like that unless provoked. You, you, you…must've provoked him! And to think that this little girl could have actually beaten my son at anything remotely intellectual is impossible," Jax said. He held up three fingers and counted them off while pointing, "I want this teacher fired, this girl expelled, and an apology from everyone involved."

"Ok, I'm sure we can work this out. AZ, why don't we start with you apologizing to Dalk?" Principal Tajek pleaded.

I opened my mouth to apologize and at the last possible moment, after the first sound escaped my mouth and the churning began in my stomach, I stopped. *Why should I apologize?*

I looked at my dad and could tell by the tortured look on his face
that he wasn't going to be leaping to my defense anytime soon. My
mother worked at Jax Robotics and Jax was her boss's boss's boss.
Dad knew Jax fired people for looking at him the wrong way. As
the family breadwinner, we couldn't afford her to lose her job. She
was probably lucky that he didn't care about employees, so he didn't
recognize our last name.

Instead, Mrs. D'Silva stepped up. "Apologize for what? For
beating him? Do you know what he does when he gets first place on
a test or wins an award? He struts. He actually struts up and down
and tells everyone within shouting distance that he's the best. But this
time he lost. AZ beat him. Fair and square. He lost and she should not
apologize for beating him."

For the second time that day, I felt a moment in my life about to
flash by. *I'm not doing what I'm supposed to be doing.* I pictured my
mother when she was being determined and slowly folded my arms.
Part of me had had enough. I've hidden my feelings and thoughts for
too long. I've put up with this kind of abuse, smiled, and stayed out
of trouble.

I don't want to live like this anymore.

Another part of me was also petrified. In this world, if you stick your neck out, it gets kicked. If you try and fail, you're a loser. You can put all the positive-attitude messages on cute pillows you like, but it doesn't change a thing.

I surveyed the room.

- Principal Tajek: Just wants all this to go away but needs Jax to be happy. Would prefer if Mrs. D'Silva resigned and I moved away.

- Mrs. D'Silva: Won't back down but doesn't want to lose her job. Wants me to stand up for myself.

- Dad: Doesn't want his wife fired. Wants me to make peace but doesn't want me to lie. Wants everyone to be happy and to be meditating.

- Jax: Wants to win. Wants his son to win. Wants everyone else to get out of the way.

- Dalk: Wants his dad to know he's still the best and to stop yelling at him. Wants me to be wrong and to beat me.

What about me? What do I want?

I want it to go away. I want no stress. But I also don't want to be bullied all the time. I'd like to be able to stand up for myself. Maybe... I'd like to win?

I remembered my mother's advice and thought about it like a puzzle:

1. I say I didn't cheat and Dalk has to live with it. No one happy. Jax pulls his school funding. Mrs. D'Silva may be fired. My life becomes hell. No.

2. I say sorry, I cheated. Jax, Dalk, and principal happy. Mrs. D'Silva and Dad disappointed. Me humiliated. No.

I have to keep my self-respect and let Dalk keep his. But how?

I got it. Option 3. Another way.

Everyone was speaking at once.

"Excuse me. Excuse me! EXCUSE ME!" I yelled. The room went quiet and every eye was on me. I normally avoided public speaking.

Am I doing the right thing?

"I will enter the robot competition this year," I said to the stillness.

"HAA HAAA HAAAAAA!" Dalk and Jax burst into an avalanche of laughter.

"*You* are going to enter the robot competition? You? Build a real robot?" Dalk asked. His eyes looked shocked, but his smirk made him seem happy.

"If Dalk is smarter than me, then he'll win and I'll lose. If I win…"

"If you win? Impossible! Dalk has won the last three years; he will win again," Jax said. "But fine, fine, enter, and when Dalk's robot crushes you, we will all see you for what you really are. Come, Dalk."

Jax and Dalk strode from the room as if they were wearing capes. I could faintly hear Jax lecturing Dalk, "You must be careful. You must win. You know what's at stake…"

"Ok. Great. All sorted then," said Principal Tajek, a relieved but anxious look on his face.

"Well done, AZ. That's a good outcome," said Dad. He patted my back and walked out of the room and back to his serenity.

"This is good. I like this version of AZ. I'd like to see more of her," said Mrs. D'Silva, unable to hide her pleasure as we both walked from the room. "And I will help you make sure you do your best."

I felt each step. Each time my foot hit the ground I felt connected to the earth.

Can this be me now? Can I do this? Well, I'm in it now.

"No, I'm not going to do my best," I said, forcing one of Mrs. D'Silva's trademark, whole-head recoils. "I'm going to win."

T-Minus Nineteen

W hen I got home, my mother greeted me with a hug and a soldering iron.

> Definition: **Solder**—A low-melting alloy, especially one based on lead and tin or (for higher temperatures) on brass or silver, used for joining less fusible metals. Used in electronics and robot building.

"I'm excited. This competition is a great idea. I've set up the workbench in the garage and sent you some links for reading," my mother said. Then she kissed my head, picked up her phone, and whooshed away, tapping ferociously.

I was born into a world of technology with my mother working for a robotics company. She always tries to get me to think like an engineer and tells me about new innovations, but I'm not sure how much has sunk in. I was lucky enough to have done some computer programming, building hardware and robotic principles at school. But actually making my own fully functioning robot was going to need much more than that.

With Mrs. D'Silva's guidance, I started with an off-the-shelf robot that I would customize. It would be basic, but it'd be easier. After a few weeks of daily work, I realized it wasn't going to be that easy.

The robot I'd picked was the YuTu 900. It was very short, and its exterior was mostly white with black sensors, nuts, and bolts. I'd seen it posted on a blog by a girl in my school named 10, who came in second place at last year's robot competition. It had:

- Three ball wheels for motion—top speed of ten miles per hour
- Nine sensors for guidance, collision detection, and facial recognition
- Voice recognition module
  - Basic speech—five thousand words
  - Basic instructions of where to go

Today I was in my garage adding the voice recognition module. I held the soldering iron with grim determination, trying hard not to let the hot metal touch my fingers as I held the tiny wire in place.

ZZZAP!

"Yowee!"

ZZAP!

I paused, sighed and looked at the soldering iron, and my now-red wrist, wondering how I ended up here.

Oh yeah. It was my idea. I'm here because of me. I got myself into this and I need to get through this. This is harder than I thought and maybe I won't win but quitting now would be way worse.

An hour later, the voice recognition module was in place and the robot lay on my worktable. I imagined I was Victor Frankenstein, about to bring my monster to life.

"Mwuu haaa haaaa haaaa," I said to the roof, quickly stopping and peering around to make sure no one had heard me. "Well, no putting it off any longer."

I needed a safe place with a flat surface to try it out. Minimal embarrassment and minimal danger. I chose an empty parking lot and the end of a rarely-used lane. It was a Wednesday afternoon and it would be empty, and its surrounding walls should contain my first experiment.

The robot was about the size of a two-year-old kid but with wheels instead of legs. I placed it down in the very middle of the rough asphalt. There was a small driveway back to the main road, a dumpster, and about five hundred disgusting cigarette butts. A few windows overlooked the scene, but no one was watching. Eyeing the dumpster, I seriously thought about picking up this clunky chunk of rubbish in front of me, throwing it in the bin, and just quitting.

I shrugged and said to my robot, "Well, what is the worst thing that can happen?"

Breathe. Breathe. Breathe.

I switched YuTu on and stood back. For a second, nothing happened. Then the little machine lit up, started whirring, and vibrated.

"It's aliiiiive!"

I really have to stop saying that.

"Command not recognized," came YuTu's reply in a flat, stop-start voice.

I raised my eyebrows and lowered myself to its height. "Hello."

"Hello," YuTu replied.

"How are you?"

"I am ready."

I thought this was a bit odd and not really what a person would say, but maybe that was a good thing. I'd thought it unlikely that anything would happen at all, so I hadn't really thought of what to do from here. "Move forward," I suggested.

The little robot made a low *ZZZ, ZZZ, ZZZ* sound and started coming forward…and kept going.

"Stop, stop, stop," I said, and the robot jerked to a stop.

"Move forward and then stop."

YuTu moved forward and then stopped.

"Spin around."

YuTu started spinning. And spinning. And kept right on spinning.

"Stop, stop, stop," I said, realizing the robot was going to take everything quite literally. I looked around the carpark, trying to think of more tests.

"I am ready," YuTu said.

"Ok, just hold on. We're going to start small. I don't want you running away from me at high speed."

"Run away at high speed," YuTu said and took off, straight down the driveway.

"Nooooooo, come back, stoppppp!" I yelled, chasing after it with my arms flapping in panic.

I reached the driveway just in time to see YuTu turn the corner onto Main Street. Then I started sprinting.

So, this is actually the worst thing that could happen.

The bustle of the street overwhelmed my senses. People, cars, shops, restaurants. My legs were burning but I was actually gaining on YuTu.

If I can just catch it…

YuTu was only just ahead of me. It turned the next corner, driven by some crazed, digital mission. I rounded the bend and entered a nightmare—the most popular café in town. About thirty people sat at the tiny wooden tables. They were unaware of their impending, metal doom.

"Stop that robot!" I yelled. Everyone turned to look at me.

I was within arm's reach of YuTu. Then, a waiter carrying a tray of food and drinks stepped out of the door of the café. I lunged forward desperately but was too late.

YuTu crashed into the waiter's legs. He buckled sideways and fell to the ground. I plowed into the waiter and the robot. The tray of drinks fell, with cakes and banana smoothies raining down on all three of us like a flurry of sweet snow. A large cappuccino landed on the waiter's lap.

"Ahh, cappuccino in my pants. Cappuccino in my pants! A robot has put cappuccino in my pants!" he yelled and yelled until the laughter of the quickly gathering crowd drowned him out.

Hoisting myself onto my elbows, I looked around at the devastation. The closest customer to us was a lady, a bit older than my mother, with a laptop covered in stickers in front of her and a look of disbelief on her face. She had a piece of chocolate cake squished on her head like an awkward hat and a river of chocolate sauce dripping down her face.

"Bravo, bravo, bravo," came a slow chant from somewhere behind her.

I saw Dalk standing above me, grinning. Then his face shifted to an exaggerated look of fear. "Well, it looks like I'm in real trouble. It's clear you have some magical ability with robots, and this is going to be a tough competition. Oh AZ, why do you persist? Why do you even try, when you already know? You do, don't you? You already know that I will win, and you will just keep embarrassing yourself."

Ok, now this is the worst thing that could have happened.

Bzzz, BZZZZ, BZZZZZZZZZZZ.

YuTu was whirring, with lights flashing and smoke streaming from multiple parts of its body.

BANG!

There was a small explosion, more smoke, and more laughter from the crowd.

Well, now at least it really can't get any worse.

"Oh dear, darling, what has happened to you? What have you done?" My mother dodged through the crowd, simultaneously panicking, apologizing, and embarrassingly wiping the waiter's pants.

"She's not normally like this," my mother said, eyes darting for cover.

Disaster.

An hour later, I was in bed, head under my pillow. Cake, smoothie, and coffee washed off. The robot in the bin. Dignity buried deep in the earth.

T-Minus Eighteen

Then came two days of humiliation at school. Dalk had surely practiced his reenactments, building to a crescendo of him lying on the ground, mimicking the waiter.

"Cappuccino in my pants, CAAAAPPUUUUCCINOOOOOO INNNNN MMYYYYY PAAANNNTTSSS! Ha ha ha ha. And then… no, wait…just listen…" His adoring fans were trying to finish the story, but this was Dalk's show. "Then her cheap robot blows up and her mother comes in to rescue poor, little *Aye Zed*." This show played over and over.

How long could this go on? Maybe if I officially pulled out of the competition, apologized, and polished Dalk's shoes for a year, he would stop? Probably not.

"It's a great first try. All the smartest people in the world had big failures early. Marie Curie got rejected from a number of universities. Come on, you can do this," my mother said after I got home from school on the second day of humiliation.

"I guess," I replied, not at all convinced.

A week after the "capu-splosion" (as it was being called), I got called to the school office because I had a visitor, which was weird. I never had visitors. I was directed into a spare office to see a lady who looked familiar.

Where have I seen her before? Oh no…it's the "cake on the head" woman from the cafe.

"Hello," the lady said. Her calm voice surprised me.

"Um, hi," I responded.

"I understand your name is AZ. I believe we briefly met last week at the café," she said.

"Um, yes, um, briefly. I'm sorry about that…cake…landing… on…your head…"

"The cake, oh yes, don't worry about that. It's the most fun I've had for a while. My name is Lucia Machado, and I was wondering if I could talk to you for a few minutes."

She wore blue jeans and a simple white blouse. Her hair was in a tight ponytail.

Well, what do I have to lose? I sat down on the chair. *Breathe. Breathe. Breathe.*

"You were testing that robot, correct?" Lucia asked.

I was a bit taken aback by her curt tone, but I had a strange urge to answer quickly.

"Yes, um, correct," I said. For some unknown reason, I felt I had to impress this lady.

"The robot is part of a school robot-building competition, correct?"

"Correct," I said, getting the hang of this conversation.

What is going on here? And where is this going?

"The competition allows teachers, parents, and coaches to support the project, but the robot must be fully built by the students, correct?"

"Correct."

"The robot can be built with a team of up to ten students, correct?"

"Correct."

"Do you want to win the competition?"

Woah, why does she want to know that?

"Correct. Umm, well, I'm not sure. I did. But it is so hard. I think I'd like to win. But it seems impossible," I said.

"All big achievements seem impossible before they are done. You shouldn't have to think about it. Do you, or don't you?" Lucia said.

I can't win this. Unless this lady has a magic wand? It would be good to win. Just for the look on Dalk's face. And the feeling of winning…it must be amazing.

Lucia was looking at me with soft eyes, clearly comfortable with silence.

I lifted my chin and looked into Lucia's eyes. "Yes," I said. "I want to win."

"Good. I would like to coach you on the project. I have a few conditions…" Lucia handed me a single sheet of paper.

> Lucia Machado will coach AZ in the school robotics competition under the following conditions:
>
> 1. You listen.
> 2. You work very hard.
> 3. You never give up.

"Now you can think about it. Think it all through and, if you accept my offer, then track me down by four thirty tomorrow and we will get started. If not, that's fine, it's your choice, goodbye and good luck," Lucia said, standing and striding out of the office like she did this kind of thing every day.

I walked back to class, still trying to work out what just happened. I had until four thirty tomorrow to find her, if I wanted to accept her offer. When I got home, I ran straight inside and searched the web.

Lucia Machado

46,624,922 results

Wow.

The first result was her Wikipedia page, which said she certainly wasn't nobody.

PhD in physics

Invented the Orbital Capacitor

Cofounder and ex-CEO of Atoki Incorporated

Founder of the Machado Foundation

Has lived in Barcelona, Rio de Janeiro, Nairobi, Sydney, Edinburgh, Austin, Shenzhen

Retired

The photo was a few years old, but her eyes beamed the same "you'd better take me seriously" look that I had seen earlier today. I kept reading for another hour.

Wow. This is someone I want on my side. Maybe she'd even give me a fighting chance to not look like a complete idiot.

I need to track her down. But how? There are no contact details on the paper. She said I had to find her before four thirty tomorrow—now I had twenty-three hours.

This is a test. I have to find her fast.

T-Minus Seventeen

I didn't find Lucia fast.

Ten hours of searching every corner of the web later, and I had nothing. Well, actually, I had a ton more confirmation that Lucia was amazing. But she was also a very private person who was difficult to reach. I submitted a "contact us" form on the website of her foundation, but that was going to be too slow.

I had messaged Mrs. D'Silva but despite knowing *of* Lucia, she didn't have any idea how to contact her.

I was running out of things to search for. My eyes felt heavy, like big, warm blankets.

"AZ…AZ…time to wake up…"

My dad's voice. I lifted my head off a hard, lumpy pillow. It turned out to be the keyboard on my computer. I could feel the imprint of keys across my face.

Well, it's only Dad.

"You were so cute, I got a photo," Dad said with a smile.

I slowly pried open my eyes to see my dad's phone with a photo of me with my face squished and my hair all over the place.

"Please, please, please delete that," I said.

"I won't share it. Maybe just with your grandparents. What were you working on?"

Rubbing my eyes, I looked up at the screen. It showed a news article about Lucia and in the comments section was my name and the following garble:

Ffjlalfjkflkjfffffffffffffffffffffffffffffffffffffffffffffffffffffffffffffffffffffff ffffffffffffffffffffffffffffffffffffffffff

Ergggggggggg, what have I done?

Then, I noticed a response below my comment.

Interesting.

Lucia Machado

"Oh no, oh no, oh no, oh no no no no no," I yelled, my hands on my cheeks.

"What? Is everything ok? Can I help?" said Dad, dropping to his knees, looking at the screen and squinting in confusion.

"No. I just need to fix this. I need to do something," I said, pushing my dad gently toward the door. Amidst more of my protests, he slowly retreated and left the room.

Lucia had responded. She'd seen this comment. Was that reaching out? Was that connecting with her? I'm not sure a garbled, forehead-written comment counted. But it was something.

Straightening up and taking a deep breath, I started typing:

Lucia, I wrote that with my head when I fell asleep. Sorry. Will you still help me?

No, that won't work. The Lucia I had just been studying wouldn't want that.

Delete.

I want to take you up on your offer. Let's get started.

Hmmm, could be stronger. What did she say yesterday? What were her conditions of working with me?

Delete…

I will listen, I will work hard, I will never give up. Let's get started.

Enter. *Blip*. Published.

I held my breath. I let it go.

Just because Lucia had commented once, didn't mean she was also at her computer, sitting there, waiting for a reply to see what—

Blip.

Reply from Lucia Machado:

Good. But you still have to track me down.

Oh wow, oh wow, oh wow.

I started typing. *Ok, thanks, but how do I track you...*

Blip.

Both replies from Lucia were gone. She'd deleted them. Of course, it wasn't going to be that easy.

8:12 a.m. Eight hours and eighteen minutes to find her. But how? I could ask Mr. Jabari, the librarian at school who seemed to know everything. School. School! It was a school day.

I don't have eight hours. I have eighteen minutes to get to school and then ninety minutes after school. Today just got harder.

An hour later, after running while eating two boiled eggs my dad had insisted I take, I was sitting in Computer Science. Mrs. D'Silva had allowed me to do a "special research project" instead of the normal schoolwork, but still I was no closer.

On my way to math, a gaggle of "cappuccino"-infused gossip stalked my periphery, but I turned on my laser focus and ignored it all. I sat forlorn in my chair and decided to actually do some math. Maybe I needed to think about something else. Leave it to my powerful subconscious.

It turned out that my subconscious was about as useful as my conscious. It was lunchtime and I had no new information, no new ideas, and fewer than four hours to go. I took off to the library.

"Mr. Jabari, do you happen to know anything about a woman named Lucia Machado?" I asked as innocently as possible at the library front desk.

"Good afternoon, AZ," said Mr. Jabari, our wonderfully friendly and constantly encouraging librarian, with his tractor-beam eye contact. "Good to see you again. I was assuming that you would be in here more often, given the big challenge you are facing. Though I thought your questions would be more about 'how to build a robot that doesn't crash,' not questions about local celebrities."

"Welllllll, she actually offered to help me, and I need to track her down as some kind of test. I was kind of hoping to find out where she lives or works…do you happen to know…either of those…maybe?" I stammered, pushing my limited influencing skills.

Mr. Jabari smiled widely and knowingly back at me. "That is great news. She would indeed be an asset. But I'm afraid Miss Machado is as private as she is brilliant. She doesn't have a mansion, despite her wealth, though I believe she has a house up in the hills. Which one though, I couldn't guess. As for work, she is retired."

My shoulders sunk from hope to despair. *Come on, give me a break here.*

"Though I have seen her around town since she moved here a few years ago. At the supermarket, at the theatre, in the park, at that Italian café…"

The cafe!

"Ok, thanks very much," I said quickly and turned to go. Seeing the hurt look on Mr. Jabari's face, I turned back and said, "And I'll be back shortly for that book you mentioned about robots."

Smiling again, he reached behind him and revealed a stack of about twelve books. "No need, I have collected some together for you."

"Um, yes, thanks for that," I said, sizing up the pile.

As the door to the library closed behind me, the end-of-lunch bell rang. I decided not to skip school. I'd go to the café straight afterward and hope Lucia was there.

Three o'clock. When the final bell rang, a victorious, barbarian horde of teenagers advanced through the hallways. I balanced the books as I was pinballed out into the real world. Awkwardly speed waddling, I made it to the café in eight minutes.

I looked to the table where Lucia had been on the day of the great robot-waiter collision, but she wasn't there. I scanned inside and outside, but no luck. I stood outside trying to think of another solution, but all I could feel was more stress.

A waiter came out of the door carrying a tray of drinks and food. He looked at me, gasped, and then heaved a sigh of relief. "No crazy robot today, *signora*?" he asked, walking past and skillfully whisking orders to customers.

Oh, he must be the cappuccino-in-the-pants guy.

"Um, hi, yes, no, no robot here today. That thing is in a bin somewhere, destined for recycling," I tried my best to smile away the nightmare. "I'm sorry about the other day."

"*Si, si*, all fine," he said, quickly stepping back inside.

3:20 p.m. Time was running out and I was running out of ideas. I was desperate, so I followed the waiter inside and found him preparing another tray of coffees.

"Um, yes, again, very sorry about that. I was wondering, that lady who was at the front table that day, with the laptop covered in stickers…"

"Ohhhh, you mean one of our best customers who ended up with a face full of cake? You mean that lady?"

"Yes, well, um, yes, her. Is there any chance you know where she lives?"

"Yes, of course. Let me get you her address straight away," he said.

My eyes lit up, then collapsed just as fast when I realized he was being sarcastic.

"Do you perhaps want to throw more cake at her?" he said.

"No, no, no, not at all. Um, in fact I would like to apologize to her, too. If possible. If that's ok?"

"Well. We don't give put customer home addresses to dangerous strangers. Sorry, you'll just have to live with the guilt. So sorry," he said, giving me a wide berth again.

Nooo. I can't be this close to some serious help and fall short.

"Erggggggggg," I said, loudly enough that a number of customers looked up at me. "Sorry."

I'd been saying that a lot lately.

One man's gaze lingered for a few seconds longer, until he returned to his laptop covered in stickers.

Lucia had a laptop like that. So what? A lot of people did. But I was running out of time and had run out of ideas. What did I have to lose? I walked up to the man's table. "Hi, um, this might sound a bit strange, but do you, um, happen to know someone named Lucia Machado?"

He flipped shut his laptop and looked at me. Then he gestured to the empty chair opposite him and I sat down. He was an older adult with a kind-looking face. "Why do you ask?"

"Well, um, well, you see, I built a robot that knocked over that waiter and dropped some cake on Lucia's head…"

The man nodded with a half-grin.

"Then she came to my school and offered to help me in this robot competition that I've entered. I've decided I want her help. I mean, I obviously need it, since my first robot is in the scrap heap. I'm trying to find out where she lives."

"If you already met her, why do you need to know where she lives?"

"Well, you see, um, she sort of told me I had to track her down."

"Ha, that's the kind of thing Lucia does. Yes, I know her. My name is Dasan, I've worked with her in the past. Let me ask you, are you sure you want her help? She can do amazing things, but she's no walk in the park. She's tough as nails. Which I'm guessing you've already worked out?"

"Oh yes, I can see that. And yes, I do want her help," I replied.

He took a breath, looked at me for a while, and then looked at the pile of books I'd placed on the table. "Well, I can see you're taking it seriously. They are mostly good books and you'll need more. Have you got a team yet? No? Well, I'm sure Lucia will help with that, too.

I'm assuming that Lucia put a time limit on you. How much time do you have?"

"Forty-two minutes," I said.

"And why do you want to enter this competition?" he asked, stroking his beard in a very cliché way.

"Well, initially it was to get out of trouble, and a bit to stop this horrible kid at my school from making my life awful, though, it will probably make things worse."

"That's not going to cut it. Not for me or for Lucia. Why else? What is going to be the impact on you if you do this?"

Who are these people and why do they ask these questions? This was my second life-changing job interview within twenty-four hours.

"Well, I guess…"

"Don't guess," Dasan snapped.

"Ok, I'll learn a lot about robots. As you said, I'll have to work in a team. And I want to beat this other kid, so I will also learn a bit about competition."

Please be the right thing to say.

I reached deep within myself. "And I want to build something. It was actually pretty amazing to turn on the robot and make it do something. I'd like to do that again."

A few seconds went by. Then he opened his laptop, typed very, very quickly for about a minute, and then looked up. "Ok, I'll help you."

Yes, yes, yes, yes, yes.

"Here is what I suggest you do. Get a takeaway double espresso, extra hot. Go get the J bus that leaves at 3:46 and get off at Hills Park. Then open this piece of paper," he said as he wrote in his notebook, tore out the page, and folded it twice.

"Can I get a double espresso, takeaway, please?" I yelled toward my non-friend waiter and reached for some money.

"I'll pay for that," said Dasan.

"Oh, thank you," I said, taking the piece of paper and putting it in my pocket. "I appreciate your help."

"Don't thank me yet. Just promise me you'll give this everything you can. And please promise me you won't ask her to repeat something. Get going," he said, extending his hand in the international signal for fist bump.

I firmly bumped him back, stood up, and put my backpack on. I picked up my books under one arm, took the cup of coffee, and strode out of the café.

3:42 p.m.

Four minutes to get to the bus station without dropping my books or the coffee. My power-waddling skills were improving dramatically.

I turned the last corner to see the bus door close.

No, come on, I'm this close. Here goes…

I stepped onto the road in front of the bus. The bus driver waved me away.

I put on an expression that said, *Oh no you don't—I'm getting on this bus whether you like it or not.*

The bus driver waved me away one more time, then shrugged and opened the door. I struggled up the stairs and fell into the first seat I found, dropping the books but managing to hold the coffee. After paying my bus fare, I regathered my composure while I watched the town go by.

You can do this. You can build a robot and make a real go at this.

4:19 p.m.

The bus pulled up at Hills Park with eleven minutes to go. I hustled off, thanking the bus driver, and put the books and coffee on the ground. I opened the piece of paper.

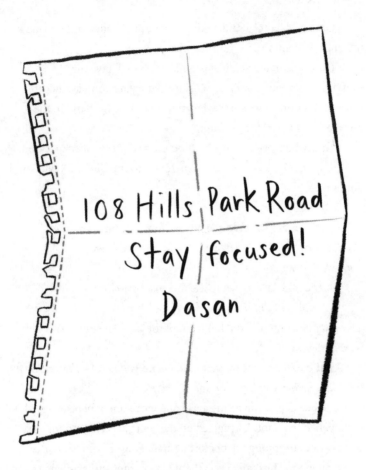

I scanned the area and saw a sign for Hills Park Road about one hundred meters away. I took off like a hasty penguin. Houses 8, 24, 42, 60, 88, 104, 106, and finally 108.

4:23 p.m.

Seven minutes to go, and I'm going to make it.

A big hedge covered the front of the house, except for a gate across the driveway. An intercom panel was camouflaged in the shrubbery, where I found a note.

The first 4 prime numbers.

> Definition: A **prime number** can be divided evenly only by two numbers: the number 1 and itself.

Another test? Are you kidding me? Ok, ok, ok, I've got this. So, 1, 2, 3, not 4 (2x2), and then 5. So, 1235.

I hit the keys and waited. *Bleeerrrr* sounded the clear signal that said "incorrect."

What? Why is that wrong? How can it be? No…ahhh. Number 1 is not considered prime by most mathematicians because it is only divisible by one number—1…so confusing. So, it is 2, 3, 5, not 6 (2x3) and 7. So 2357.

4:29 p.m.

I hit the keys at pace and waited…

Clink! Whirrrrr.

The gate opened inward. I rushed in, down a path and up to the front door, about to knock (it down). Another note.

Surely not another puzzle?

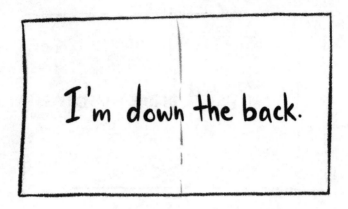

I quickly walked down another path beside the house. I came to a beautiful garden, with flowers, trees, and a pond with a bridge. Seeing nowhere else to go, I raced over the bridge. It took me between two trees which opened up into a sun-filled clearing. In the middle, on a wooden bench seat, sat Lucia, reading a huge book.

I skidded to a halt in front of her. "Found you!" I said, like we were playing hide and seek.

Lucia looked at her watch, placed a bookmark in her book, and looked me up and down.

"Is that a double espresso?" she asked, almost smiling.

T-Minus Sixteen

L ucia sipped her coffee, legs crossed at the knee, floral skirt almost touching the ground. She tapped her free hand on her knee.

What do I do now?

A full minute went by.

"So, can you help me?" I asked.

Lucia picked up a red notebook beside her and wrote while she narrated:

More patience and comfort with silence.

What? More comfort with silence? What's that supposed to mean? And more patience? It's been a minute at least, maybe five, how long do I have to be patient for? I should ask her. Actually, that's not a very patient thing to do.

With great effort, I closed my mouth and tried very hard to wait.

More notes were added into the red book:

Learns quickly.

"Oh, thanks, that's great," I beamed.

Before I'd even finished the sentence, Lucia struck a line through the last note with a brutal *fffwweeck* of her pencil:

Learns quickly.

I held in a heavy sigh. I won the battle, but only just.

"Ok. Here we are. I'm glad you found me. This is going to be an interesting challenge and I haven't had one of those for a while. For clarity, you are going to be the biggest part of that challenge. If I solve you, the rest will be easy. But you will challenge me. Oh yes you will," Lucia said. Her voice was like a marching band. It had a friendly beat but hurried you along.

"Um, ok, thank you, I guess," I responded.

"The time for guessing has passed. We must act. Yes?"

"Um, yes, I gue…sorry. Yes," I finished with a bit more certainty.

"Let's walk," Lucia said, finishing her coffee and striding down the path.

I left my books on the bench and hurried to catch up to the sprightly woman.

"Why are we here, AZ?" Lucia asked.

"Here? In your garden?"

"No, why are you and I here together? Why is this thing happening? This competition?"

"Well, the short version is that I beat this guy named Dalk solving a puzzle at school and he didn't like it. So, his dad yelled at Principal Tajek and I said I'll enter the robot competition. My first test robot dropped a piece of cake on your head, and then you turned up at my school offering to help, then I tracked you down and here we are."

Without slowing down, Lucia added to her red notebook:

Better storytelling.

"Yes, but why? Why did you beat him? Why did you choose the robot competition as the way to pacify the situation?"

"Well, I beat him because he insulted me, and I chose the competition because it seemed the easiest way out."

"No, wrong on both counts. He'd insulted you before, surely, and entering a robot competition is not easy at all. Try again."

"Well…"

"Enough with all these 'well's and 'so's, just say what you want to say," Lucia said, not looking at me.

"W—" I took a sharp intake of breath and, with my chin up, said, "I was sick of it. Sick of him saying he is so smart and winning all the time."

"Especially when…"

"When what? I don't know what you want me to say,"

"I think you do. We can't proceed until you say it," Lucia said, "He insulted you. He thinks no one is as smart as him. He always wins. And out of all the students in the class, it made you angry enough to act. You were the only one who did. What made you so angry? What made you do something when for years you had done nothing but sit back and take it?"

Why is she doing this?

"I was just angry, so I tried..."

"No. That's not it. You know why. You were the only one who did something, why?" Lucia walked faster now, her words as crisp as the air.

I stopped, hit my clenched fists against my thighs and yelled, "Because I'm smarter than him!" My breath came in gasps, sounding loud amongst the quiet trees.

Lucia walked toward me, crouched down, and looked up into my watery eyes with a wicked smile. "Yes. Yes, you are."

T-Minus Fifteen

The next Saturday morning I was at a nearby sports field, watching a girl warm up for soccer. Her name was 10, which was also the number on her jersey. I don't think 10 was the name written on her birth certificate, but it was what she wanted the world to know her by. It was pronounced "ten," written as 10, and never, ever referred to as a nickname. Her teammates and the other team had arrived—the game was about to start.

"We've got this. This game is ours," 10 said to her teammates, as the referee blew her whistle.

I sat nearby under some trees and watched 10 play. She was really good. Tough, but her team definitely respected her.

When the game finished, I waited as 10 sat on the sideline in the shade, chatting with her team.

Lucia had said I need a team. I can't do it all on my own. 10 had come second to Dalk three years in a row and was my obvious first choice.

From reading her fairly extensive blog, I learned that soccer was her preferred sport and her only form of meditation. In one post, she wrote: "When I lace up my boots, I enter another world. The grass, the lines, the goal posts, the nets, and the big open space. The wonderful empty."

The rest of the team finally went home and 10 sat alone, looking up at the sky.

"Did you win?" I asked, approaching the shade of the tree.

10 looked up at me.

"I wondered if you would come and talk to me," 10 said, shading her eyes from the sun. "I assumed you would make a minimal effort, take the inevitable and painful boasting from Dalk for the rest of your school life, and then move away as far away as possible. But you're here talking to me. You're actually taking it seriously."

"Um, yes. Yes, I am."

"Great. Best of luck to you," 10 said.

"But I can't do it alone. I'd like you to join my team. Together I think we could win."

She laughed a bit and then stared at me for ten seconds.

"I'd like to join your team," 10 finally said, with a firm nod of her head.

"That's great, I really think that we—" I said as 10 raised a flat hand to stop me.

"I'd like to..." 10 continued, "but I won't. For two main reasons. One, because I really don't care. And two, technically, you can't beat him. You just can't. He has money. Resources. Support. It's not Dalk that wins that competition, it's Jax Enterprises—one of the world's leading robotics companies. I didn't just come second. I came a way, way, way, nearly there, way, way, way back second. Ok, technically, three reasons. Three, I am not going to be humiliated again. I'm not even entering this year. What's the point?"

10 got up, shoved her things in her bag, and turned to leave.

"We can beat him," I said.

"You can't," 10 replied over her shoulder.

"We can," I repeated.

"There is no 'we.' "

T-Minus Fourteen

The Private Blog of 10

I just got back from soccer. As I guessed, AZ came and asked me to help her build a robot. I said no.

Two hours and one short shower later, I was in my lab. The screen showed what looked like multicolored, oddly formatted gibberish on a black background. I knew what it meant and so did my computer. It was code. A program for my robot.

My headphones found their home over my ears and my world filled with jazz music. I closed my eyes, took a breath, and started coding. Less than five minutes in, I was rudely interrupted by my own thoughts.

Don't even think about it. There's no way it makes a difference to work with AZ. Ok, maybe a tiny difference, but not enough. Forget about it. Back to coding.

She seems pretty determined. I wonder why? It'd be so good to wipe even just a bit of that smirk off Dalk's face…

I watched the video of last year's robot competition. I thought I had him. But he had me. Completely had me. I paused the video with the smile on his face and a look of shock on my face. I gave it everything. I lost.

A ping pulled me out from my sorrow, and I opened my messages. It was AZ. She had gotten my number from a girl in our class.

AZ: I can't do this without you.

10: He's beaten me three years in a row. Technically smashed me.

AZ: Yes, he's beaten you three times. But if you quit now, he wins forever.

10: You saw last year's final. It was my best and it was way short.

AZ: It wasn't your best. You know Moore's Law?

10: Yes. Computing power doubles every 2.5 years. So what?

AZ: Think about it, every year, your robot-building ability doubles too. Remember two years ago?

10: Maybe… IDK.

AZ: You double. Trust me. What if you had resources like Dalk?

10: Sure, that would be great. You plan on winning the lottery? You know that gambling is technically a tax on people who are bad at math?

AZ: You said there is no "we" but there is a "we."
There's already a team. Mrs. D'Silva has been really
supportive from the start and now Lucia Machado is
helping me.

10: The crazy loner who lives in the hills? Great. Now
our problems are solved.

AZ: When you've got money, you're eccentric,
not crazy.

AZ sends me a link to Lucia Machado's Wikipedia page.

10: Wow. She's done some stuff.

AZ: Yes, she's done some stuff and she's offered to
help me, but she says I need a team. A good team...

AZ: We need you.

10: ...

AZ: ...

10: ...Even if we had support, why would I go through
all the work just to probably lose again?

AZ: I can't answer that, but I'll tell you why I'm doing
it. Every year for as long as I can remember, I've seen
guys like Dalk win these competitions with a smile on
their face like they're entitled to it; it's as if they're just
breezing through life. I'm smart, I work hard, but I've
never even tried to go up against them. But I'm doing
it now because I want to know, if I work in a great
team, and give it all I've got, that I can be just as good.
Maybe I can even do something amazing. We can do
it together.

10: ...

AZ: They say you regret the things you don't do much more than the things you do. I don't want to be a grumpy seventy-year-old saying that maybe I could have done something awesome if I had just tried and not given up.

Five minutes go by.

10: ...

AZ: ...You still there?

10: Yes, I'm still here. I'm just thinking.

AZ: Ok, just checking... :)

10: Here are my conditions.

AZ: YES!

AZ: YES!

AZ: YES!

10: Calm down, I haven't said yes yet. You need to hear my conditions first.

AZ: Anything, I'll do it.

10: Condition one.

AZ: I love it! It's fine, I'm in.

10: AZ, really?

AZ: Sorry, go ahead.

10: Ok, now I need a new condition one, which is you need to exercise a bit more restraint with your enthusiasm. Just a healthy amount, ok?

AZ: 🤖 Affirmative.

10: Condition two: We are a team till we agree the team is over.

AZ: Done. Of course.

10: Condition three: We do good. Our work helps, not hurts. We don't make an evil robot Skynet-style or add features like drone missiles.

AZ: We're just making one normal robot! But yes, of course, never. No Skynet. No drone missiles. No robotic Jar Jar Binks, either, just saying.

10: Agreed. No Jar Jar. Let's make that condition four.

AZ: Yep, that's good.

10: So, what do we do first?

AZ: We get to work!

Day One of Working with AZ

AZ and I get to work. We work in my lab after school during the week and most of the weekend. We have 22.8 weeks until the competition. Her mother and dad came to visit us and check out our workspace. Her mother knew her stuff about the equipment but spent most of the time on her phone. Her dad just asked about safety. They seemed happy enough to let AZ work here with me.

After they left, we addressed some big
questions from AZ:

"So why have you lost for three years in a row?" AZ
asked, reading off of a notebook.

Ouch.

"Too slow, too 'last year,' too boring," AZ said, really
laying it on.

Triple ouch!

"But mostly because it was too predictable."

*Hmmm, she's right. Dalk knew what was coming and
was ready for every move. How do we change that?*

Day Two—Robot Version 1.01

We've finally agreed on the plan for the new robot. No
more off-the-shelf for AZ, we're starting this one from
scratch. And no more R2D2 style; we are going for a
full humanoid.

For three years, I've worked alone. Jazz music
tumbling out of the speakers fitting in nicely with the
zzzt, zzzt, beep, crash of my tools.

Now I have someone to work with. AZ's been
cramming on her programming and hardware skills.
They're not bad, she's no veteran, but at least she's
useful. The saying goes that two coders doesn't mean
a project is done in half the time. But they also say that
two people should feed off each other to produce a better
result. At least that's the idea.

I think this is going to be much better.

Day Three—Robot Version 1.02

This is much worse.

This is just out-and-out frustrating. Why does she do so many annoying things? The spacebar on her laptop appears to be spring-loaded and she *clack, clack, clacks* it out all day long. She's constantly leaving her soldering iron on. She likes to play '80s music as "it helps me concentrate." And she's always saying, "Ok, great," fifty times a day. Aaargh.

Worst of all, after putting up with this all day long, she says to me, "Do you have to do that?"

"Oh, please, tell me what I am doing to annoy you?" I say, with some of my best sarcasm.

"Well, your keyboard has a broken key that goes *duh*," AZ starts, but then, if you can believe it, she goes on, "Also, you keep getting slowed down because you have to wait five minutes for your soldering iron to warm up, and, your music sounds like random instruments, finally, you say 'technically' eight times an hour," she outlines so wonderfully.

My keyboard? My soldering iron? My music? My annoying phrases? Are you kidding me?

This may be the shortest-lived partnership in history. I'll give it one more day.

Day Four—Robot Version 1.05

Twelve minutes into work, we are yelling at each other. We both walk out, then I realize this is my lab and I walk back in. Then I remember how angry I am and walk out again.

Oh well, back to the old days of working alone.

Day Six—Robot Version 1.08

I haven't handled this as well as I could. I'm about to send AZ an instant message saying I'm sorry when she sends me the same message first.

We agree to try again. We meet up in the lab and get to work. I almost say something about *her* soldering iron, but I catch myself, take a deep breath, and keep working. I notice her do the same thing a few times.

It's not easy, but we made some good progress today.

Day Seven—Robot Version 1.09

Today was hard. We started working on the motherboard early on Saturday morning, but quickly got stuck.

> Definition: A **motherboard** is a printed circuit board containing the principal components of a computer or other device.

Here's the problem. There are *a lot* of components we need to put on the robot's motherboard:

1. CPU—Central processing unit

2. Timer—The clock that controls synchronization

3. Voice—The chip that controls voice activation

4. Graphics—What gets displayed on the screen

5. Machine learning—How the computer learns to think

6. NLP (natural language processing)—Helps the computer understand normal, human language

7. Heat sinks—Keeps motherboard cool

8. Power connector—Provides power from the batteries into the motherboard

9. Memory slot—Stores data the motherboard needs to access quickly

10. Communications chip—Manages communications in and out of the motherboard

For maximum cooling, because the motherboard gets hot, hot, hot, we need to space out the components as much as possible with no overlapping. We also don't want it to be too big. In fact, it has to stay very small and fit into a square about the size of a piece of bread:

The Motherboard Puzzle

This is the space all the other components need to fit into.

These are all the components that need to fit onto the motherboard. (Cut this page out at the end of the book!)

We tried fourteen variations in the morning—the parts didn't fit.

We tried twenty-six variations in the afternoon—they still didn't fit.

We tried thirty-nine variations that night—they *still* didn't fit.

After checking in with our parents, we decided to push through all Friday night until we solved it.

2:18 a.m. We were cold. Hungry. Tired.

We got it. *Every piece perfectly fit on the motherboard.* We did it.

AZ got up from where she was hunched on her stool and did a little dance. Or what might be interpreted as a dance. It wasn't pretty. Her knees were going out at diagonals. Her head was swaying side to side. She was pointing her pinky fingers up to the sky. All the while turning in a slow circle.

I watched for a mortified second. Then I did the unthinkable. I started dancing, too. It must have been the endorphins. That's the only logical explanation.

> Definition: **Endorphins** are hormones that interact with the receptors in your brain and reduce your perception of pain. Endorphins also trigger a positive feeling in the body.

A few minutes later, we were both laughing till our stomachs hurt. AZ finally caught her breath and walked over to me with her hand raised in the universal signal for "give me a high five."

AZ said, "That was, um, good."

"Yeah, good," I reply, but I'm thinking, *Good? That was heart-grindingly terrible until thirty minutes ago, and now it's crazy amazing.* But I high-five her back to not leave her hanging. It's awkward, but it's a start. Back to building.

Day Twenty-Four—Robot Version 1.26

After more than three weeks of working in our lab, AZ and I are nearly ready for our first real test.

Lucia is in my lab guiding us. Sometimes she looks around, says a very cryptic comment, like, "Urgent is not always important," or, "In soccer, don't you have to go backward to go forward sometimes?" and then leaves.

She's a bit weird, but she has also helped. She lent us some really new, cutting-edge equipment which has made our robot building at least 2.8 times as good. She's also connected us to robotics experts at some big companies (though not Jax Enterprises, which she despises).

Tomorrow, we do our first field test.

T-Minus Thirteen

After weeks of work, 10 and I brought our new robot to school. The aim was to test it in as close to the final environment as possible, and with the school hall closed, my dad suggested that the school playground was the next best option. I was just happy to avoid anything public or coffee related.

In one of our toughest debates, we had finally settled on a name for the robot. With all my reading and a few conversations over breakfast with my mother, I knew what I wanted, so I put together a pretty slick presentation, including photos. I stood in front of 10 and argued my case…

"10, let me tell you a story about a computer programmer. Hear me out. Ada Lovelace, born in 1815, is encouraged to learn mathematics and logic by her mother to try and stop her going nutso like her dad supposedly did. Not only is she *not* nutso, but she's wicked smart and awesome. How awesome? A lot. Count this up for me:

"One, at age twelve, she decides she wants to fly and writes a book with designs, materials, and the anatomy of birds.

"Two, at age seventeen, she gets introduced at the Royal Court of England and meets the world's best scientists and is referred to as a 'brilliant mind.' Remember, this is an age when women can't vote and have very few rights.

"Three, at age twenty-seven, she translates a mathematical paper from Italian into English and in her notes, she outlines an algorithm by which a computer could do calculations. This is commonly referred to as the first-ever computer program. (First post! Yipee!)

"Four, she also contemplates artificial intelligence and says her computer would never originate anything. (Reminder, she was twenty-seven and this is 150 years ago…so we can let this one go.)

"Five, she was witty, strong, courageous, and she persisted despite being constantly against all odds.

"I'd like to honor her by naming our robot Ada (though of course, our robot will not have a gender; it's a robot, not a person)."

10 was quiet for about a minute. "Ok, yes, Ada it is. I mean, how am I supposed to argue with that? And that was actually pretty good. You're getting better at this stuff."

With Ada ready to meet the world for the first time, we got to school at six thirty, which would give us a full hour before anyone else arrived. I rubbed my hands together quickly and 10 rubbed her eyes.

With Ada lying in the middle of the playground, 10 and I fist bump for luck, with nervous smiles on our faces.

This is a big moment. I know it. 10 knows it. Somehow even Ada knows it.

From her laptop, 10 ran the initializing program. Ada's lights came on, with some low-level hums, a few beeps, and then Ada spoke.

"Hello," said Ada in a slow, computerized voice.

I looked at 10 and smiled. So far, so good. We ran the second series of programs to test motion. Ada stood up slowly and took a few awkward first steps. Wobbled. But stayed up. Turned, wobbled again, stepped, wobbled, and fell over. We helped Ada up and tried again. Steps, wobbles, wobbles, turns, wobbles, steps and stops.

10 and I both let out a deep breath at the same time. The look on 10's face said "not great, but not bad." 10 ran the third program, where we tested Ada's conversation skills.

"Hello," said Ada.

"Hello, Ada. It's wonderful to meet you," I said.

"Hello, what is your name?" Ada asks in a cliché robotic, jumpy voice. The voice needs some work.

"My name is AZ, how are you?" I ask, smiling.

"Me. Good," Ada says.

This will be historic. I need to say something profound.

"Ada, I want to tell you that you are an amazing robot and you can do amazing things. We have big hopes for you and whatever it is you want to do; you can do it."

"Yes. Me. Can. Do. It," Ada says, leaving me with a feeling of anti-climax.

The tests are going well, and time is limited, so 10 suggests running a combo test of program two and three. Walking and talking.

"It's time to step it up," 10 says to Ada.

Ada started walking in the square formation again.

"Ada, what is your favorite color?" I ask.

"My favorite color is gray," Ada says.

I smile at the answer. Boring, but a start. "Ada, what is the nearest planet to earth?"

"The nearest planet to earth is earth," Ada replied, taking a turn and surviving another wobble.

"She's technically correct, I guess, but the AI needs some work too. Um, is Ada moving a bit faster than she's supposed to be?" 10 asks.

I shrugged and continued on. "Ada, what is the square root of—"

"Me can do it," Ada interrupted, definitely going faster.

"I'm looking at the logs, yes, something is going on," 10 said, typing.

"Yes, you can do it, but slow down and we can—" I said.

"ME CAN DO IT. ME CAN DO IT. ME CAN DO IT," Ada
chanted at full volume and didn't stop on one of the corners and
headed straight for a wall. A collision at this pace could do a lot
of damage.

10 pinged her keyboard at ludicrous speed. At the last second,
Ada did a 270-degree pivot but kept going, missed the wall but
hit a tree.

"ME CAN DO IT. ME CAN DO IT. ME CAN DO IT." Ada's
legs and arms walked forward but her face and body were stuck on
the tree. Dirt flew and leaves swirled. 10 madly typed on her laptop to
bring Ada under control, but it didn't work.

I decided to risk serious injury by turning off Ada's main power.
I ran, leaped, and got hit with an arm across my back that really hurt.
With another dodge and a bit of luck, I turned Ada off.

Without power, Ada slowed down, lost balance and fell back.
I caught Ada, like in a trust fall. With Ada cradled in my arms,
face dented and scratched, covered in dirt and tree fragments, I
started to cry.

I smelt the acrid burning of electronics and I heard 10's labored
breath. I looked over and through my tears saw 10 doubled over,
vomiting on the dirt.

"Annnnnnnnd cut," we heard someone yell from behind us.

A window in one of the classrooms was open and a camera
lens poked out. The lens disappeared back into the void, and a head
appeared. It was Dalk.

"I couldn't have planned it better myself. Thank you," Dalk said
with a look of appreciation on his face. "When I heard you two were
teaming up against me this year I thought, 'Should I be worried?' The
answer, of course, is no. Now if you'll excuse me, I need to go put this
on the internet."

Dalk smiled and looked at me, lying on the ground holding Ada.
I'd stopped crying. My eyes, like my breath, were still and clear. I
stared at him, through him, with all my love of Ada and all my spite.

Dalk's smirk disappeared, he looked down at the ground, fidgeted with his camera, and quickly turned and walked away.

I turned back toward Ada.

"Ada, this competition is no longer about just surviving it. This is too important. You're too important."

I was ready to take this up a level.

T-Minus Twelve

The next day, 10 and I sat with Lucia in her garden.

"Yes, I get what happened. I'm asking *why* it happened?" Lucia asked.

"Well, technically, Ada's systems were—" 10 said.

"I'm not talking about the technical mistakes; I'm asking why they happened at all? And ignoring the crash, how did Ada seem?"

"Ada was also fairly stiff…too robotic, which I know sounds funny. But to win we have to be smooth. And the crash? Well, we missed something. A few things," I said.

"Yes, you missed something. I think you're missing something… Someone. The team isn't complete yet," Lucia said.

10 looked at me and back to Lucia, "Missing someone? Really? What do you mean?"

"I mean your team needs someone else to really do something amazing. You two seem enough to get the job done, but you need more than that. You need something special."

10's lip curled at the edge and she gave a shrug.

"It's simple in principle and complex in action," Lucia said. "You are both working well together. You complement each other. 10 has the technical depth and AZ has the purpose, while developing her leadership and technical skills. The team is functionally good. Functional is great to build something you already know how to build. But it's not going to build something more than that. For that, you need creativity and what they call the X-Factor. You need some positive friction."

"Ok, so how do we get some 'positive friction'?" I asked.

"Well, who in your school is different? Really different. Someone who can take this to a whole new plane of thinking."

"Different. How about really, really, really different?" I said looking at 10 with an eyebrow raised.

"No. No way. Not Li," 10 said, shaking her head.

"I like this reaction. Tell me more," Lucia said.

"There is an artsy student who would definitely be described as kinda different, named Li," I said.

"Kinda different? More like giga-strange," 10 said. "Li does everything opposite. If the obvious thing to do is to go left, Li will go right. If everyone has to wear green, Li will wear orange. If we all have to do a project where you need to write twenty pages, Li will do a five-word poem. Li…Li…oh no, I'm describing the person you want, aren't I?"

"Yes," I said with Lucia nodding. "Let's go see if Li's up for a challenge."

The next day, 10 and I were walking down the road in another part of our town. My gaze was sternly toward the horizon and my strides purposeful. 10 was looking at the clouds, her strides all at angles, like she wanted to turn and run.

"Are we really doing this?" 10 asked.

"Yes. We are. We need a third kind of thinking—a third kind of heat—if we are going to win this thing," I said.

"Ok, as you know, I love your new level of competitiveness. You're sneering a lot more than you used to, which is awesome, it really is. But technically, we don't agree all the time and why do we have to be revolutionary?" 10 asked.

"Yes, we disagree on things like which component to use, which structure, using tabs or spaces, if it's pronounced 'gif' or 'jif' (it's gif, BTW), but they are minor. We need someone to think differently about the big stuff. And yes, we do need to be revolutionary. Dalk doesn't just put the same robot up each year, his robot gets better and better. Significantly. Massively. If we are going to win—and we *are* going to win—then we need to get exponentially better."

> Definition: **Exponential growth** is when something grows by a factor of 10. Instead of growing linearly like 10, 20, 30, 40, 50, exponential growth is 10, 100, 1,000, 10,000.

"So where are we going, technically?"

"Um, I kind of don't really know, but I'm also kind of hoping that we'll find Li somewhere at the park? I have seen Li here a few times."

We walked around the park for twenty minutes without any sign of Li.

"Can't we just talk to Li at school tomorrow?" 10 said.

"Hello," came a voice from above.

10 and I both turned and looked up into the tree we were standing under. Reclining in the crook of a branch was Li, holding an orange peel that looked to be shaped like a spider.

"Hello," Li said. "Do you happen to know what color it is, please?"

"I'm just so glad we found you," I said with a sigh of relief.

"I'm glad you're glad, but I'm pretty sure that I found you," Li responded.

"Um, yes, I guess so. And, sorry, what was it you asked, what time it is?"

"Interesting. No, I don't much care for time. I'm very curious to know what color it is."

I noticed Li's voice for the first time. It was like a pixie's melody. Almost singing, almost asking something. I looked at 10, whose face seemed to say, *This is a huge mistake, can we please get away from this person as fast as possible?*

"Um, what color is *what*?" 10 asked.

"Just the color. If you had to say, today, right now, if it was a color, what would it be?"

I shrugged, looked around, took a breath and took a chance. *Could all of this really hang on a color?*

"Definitely light purple."

Li suddenly hid the spider-peel in a pocket somewhere and jumped down to the ground next to 10 and I.

"Light purple, you say?" Li asked. "Interesting."

Li smiled broadly, grabbed my hand, and lifted it to look at my elbow for about forty-five seconds. I looked to 10 for guidance and was about to pull my arm away. Li hummed a tune and, seemingly satisfied, let go of my arm. Li then sat down on the grass, fingers slowly trawling through the blades, eyes closed.

"So, um, 10 and I," I said, "we are, um, we have, entered a competition, the school robot-building competition."

Li found a leaf on the ground, and lifting it up, held it close as if listening to it.

"And *we* were kind of wondering…" I said, while 10 pointed at me mouthing *you*, "*We* were wondering if maybe it would be good to have a bigger team to work on it and get some different ideas. Different perspectives. Different everything."

Li's hands mimed pulling air from all directions.

"So, we thought maybe, that you could join our team and help us build a really amazing robot. The team is really only 10 and I. And our robot, Ada, of course, which is three. You'd be four. Though we have a mentor as well, plus Mrs. D'Silva and Mr. Jabari are helping too. 10 has built lots of robots and I'm learning, fast. We'd really like you to help us make the robot different."

Li took a leaf, tore it in two, releasing the smell of mint, eating one half and throwing the other half into the air.

"It's going to be really fun and we could win, but it's also going to be really hard, and we also might lose…" I continued.

Oh my, I don't even believe myself here. How do I get Li excited about this?

Li's tongue began to make a clicking noise, with absolutely no pattern whatsoever.

"So, do you want to join our team?" I asked, my voice trailing off.

Li rubbed the tips of four fingers on each hand against each other, smiling.

A minute passed.

"Yes," Li said.

10 and I looked up in unison.

"What?" I asked.

"Huh?" 10 asked.

"Yes, I'd like to join your team to build roberts," Li said.

"Ro-bots. Building ro-bots," 10 said.

"Yes, robots, too," Li said.

"Really, that's great. But it's robots, ok? You get that, right?" I asked.

"Yes. It doesn't really matter. I was hoping for something different to do today, and this smells much curious," Li said.

"Smells much curious? Is that like 'sounds good'?" 10 asked.

"Not really, not at all, but it's a happy thing. Just in case your face, all bunchy-up as it is, is worried it's an unhappy thing." Li said.

I know this seems even crazier now, but we need a bit of crazy.

"Two clouds are floating around me," Li said, holding up both hands, one flat and one angled, which looked nothing like clouds. "The first cloud says, 'What is the thing that you said which is called a robot competition?' "

"Um, hey, yes, that's a good question Li, or cloud, both of you, thanks," I said. "Let me tell you how it works."

Li gently patted the grass. I slowly and awkwardly sat down. 10 crossed her arms while Li kept patting. 10 threw her arms up in the air and joined us on the grass.

"So, um, a robot competition is, well, a competition to build the best robot. Anyone from the school can enter, your team can be up to ten people, you can get support from parents and teachers, but the robot must be built by the students," I said.

"Fascinating. Just fascinating. And you're saying that this happens in our school?' Li asked.

"Yes, it happens every year. Haven't you seen it?" 10 asked. "The big finale where all the robots compete?"

"Not yet. But go on," Li said.

"Ok, so, um, the robots have to perform three challenges and they change each year," I explained. "The better you do in each round, the more points you get. Whichever robot has the most points after the three rounds, wins."

Li's mouth opened, as if about to say something, but nothing came out.

I waited a few seconds, then continued, "So we are building a robot and the competition is tough so it won't be easy, and we might come last, but we are kind of hoping that we could just maybe… possibly…win…maybe."

"Don't hold back on those confidence levels AZ, we don't want to get too excited," 10 said.

"Well, I don't want to set the wrong expectation. It's going to be hard. And I know this is new for Li," I said.

Then Li started singing:

"Hard is good and I love new,
Plus, the *robot* competition, too,
Challenges to win, rounds to earn,
It's a rainbow day when I get to learn."

10 and I looked at Li in silence, then 10 started smiling.

"What's so funny?" I asked 10.

"Technically, everything. Everything about this is funny. Ludicrous, but funny," 10 said.

"Yes, hilarious. Now, let's talk more about our plans," I said.

"That would be good. I just have one more question, please," Li asked.

"Sure, what is it?" I asked.

"What is a robot?"

T-Minus Eleven

A Letter to Li's Grandmother

Dear Grandmother Blossom, from your Loving Beam of Joy, Li,

I have news to share which will hopefully make you see orange, your third favorite color. I have become a member of an adventurous band of teenagers on a wild and crazy journey. This trio, for there are three of us, was formed just 17,580 minutes ago and, in that time, my world has been wonderfully turned into another kaleidoscope. I also risked my life for the first time, which was thrilling.

This group has entered a robot competition. There are two things about this I would like to share. The first one: a robot is a mechanical, computerized machine that can do things you want it to do. I am truly amazed. Young people like us, entrusted with screwdrivers, wires, and microchips (very small computer parts) can be combined in the right way to create magic. To create life. I am astounded. I am changed.

And two: a competition is where multiple groups try to be better than each other according to a set of rules. It sounds all quite Neanderthal but I am assured there is no physical battle that transpires.

Truly, I didn't know anything about either of these before I started, and even more truly, I'm still working it out.

Let me tell you about the other members of our team; AZ and 10—how wonderful are those names?

AZ.

She is wonderful.

She is outwardly and inwardly wrestling and debating; she challenges demons, has confidence and anxiety, humility and desire. What will happen if she fails? Or, perhaps more confronting, what will happen to the world if she succeeds?

What fascinates me the most is how she can make something from seemingly nothing. Atoms and space, in happy combination, by her orchestra of gray cells, play in harmony. Yes, she is a conductor.

I will help her on her journey.

10.

She is a treasure.

Imagine a cactus. That has needle-sharp, frozen icicles for thorns, and yet still shirks away from touch or light or love. You could paint that so well; I can see it! Now imagine that cactus in the sun. Warmed, thawing, opening up, thorns transmogrifying into clouds—transmogrify means to transform or alter something in a magical, surprising way.

When 10 talks to her computer, it really listens to her. She likes that it does. It is the closest thing to alchemy I've seen—turning base materials into magic. 10 has tried, through a sea of sighs, to teach me how it all works, and this is how my mind sees this mysticism:

1. You write down one million characters, in ten thousand lines in exactly the right sequence, which is a computer program.

1. Then another program, like a translator but called a compiler, rewrites everything into ones and zeros, which is the only language computers actually understand.

1. Then you put that program into a robot's body (made up of wires).

1. And if everything is done exactly right, the robot works.

Like me, you may need a long walk after that story. It's a world within worlds that creates worlds.

10 is not ready for a long hug. Not yet. Not yet.

Lucia.

There is also Lucia who is helping us. She reminds me a lot of you, Blossom, except she is almost completely and utterly the opposite. Lucia was once helped, and so, wants to help, which is a smile.

It was Lucia who suggested we learn more about our competition (they are the people trying to beat us and we're supposed to not like them, but as you know, I love everyone). We all went over to the lab where Dalk (who is like the big bad wolf) builds his robots.

We were watching from across the road for about five minutes and not seeing anything except the front door, when I got up and crossed the road. AZ and 10 jumped up, screamed at me, and suggested I turn around. I did not. They hid. I walked in the front door and then this is what happened.

I walked directly into Dalk, who I'd seen at school but never spoken to. He not-very-politely asked, "What are you doing here, weirdo?" If only he knew how wonderful being weird was.

After a short conversation and some laughter, he invited me to his lab to see his robot called Ukko. I saw it, nodded as I've seen others do when they are taking something quite seriously, and then went and told AZ and 10 what I saw.

AZ went from disappointment, to sadness, to despair. 10 went from smirking, to laughing, to ROTFLSMMUHFOAIDMFS—which means Rolling On The Floor Laughing So Much My Unicorn Horn Fell Off And I Dropped My Falling Star, except this time without the unicorn or star.

I took a few moments and thought, "What would Grandmother do?" and held their hands in mine.

Then I said, "We will be better."

And we will.

Well, that is enough stories for one letter. I hope to hug you soon.

Much love from your gentle, swaying in the grass,

Li

T-Minus Ten

The day after Li met Ukko, the three of us gathered in Lucia's study and told her what happened.

"So what now?" Lucia asked the cool lab air.

I just don't know. What if we go through all this and don't even get close? What if I let everyone down?

"What now? Well, I thought it was going to be very hard but doable. Now it just doesn't seem possible. So, it would save everyone a lot of time and effort if we just quit," I said.

"Technically, yes, you can quit. Realistically? Not so much," 10 said without looking up.

She's right, if I quit now, it would actually be worse than losing.

"Is that what you want to do?" Lucia asked.

"No, but I wish I could," I replied.

"Logic is like sandpaper. It can smooth the edges, but it can never make anything new," Lucia replied.

"Bravo!" Li yelled, shocking everyone. "I'd quite like to win this robot competition please. Can someone please tell me what actually happens in the competition?"

"Ok, sure, so there are three parts to the competition, held over three days," I said.

"Three parts, three days, I like it," said Li.

"**Part one** of the competition is the creative section. Each robot has to perform for three minutes and demonstrate as much creativity as possible. There are three judges who can award you five points maximum for five areas, which are creativity, content, movement, crowd participation, and crowd appreciation." I put the list onto the board.

1. Creative- How different, diverse, artistic, new, unique
2. Content- The nature of the subject and material
3. Movement- Total robot movement, elegance and style
4. Crowd participation- How much the crowd got involved
5. Crowd appreciation- How much cheering and applause was recieved

"The robot can dance, juggle, do magic, sing, or tell jokes. It's up to you," I said.

"Or stand perfectly still?" Li suggested.

"Brilliant. So creative! Though, they may just think we didn't power it up?" said 10, snapping her fingers to drive home the sarcasm.

"Probably not stand still, but, hey, it's different, very different," I said.

"Part two?" asked Lucia.

"Yes, **part two** is the mental section. Five riddles, puzzles, or trick questions are asked of the robot and each is worth five points. The questions get harder and harder as you go along. It tests the robot's cognitive functions, AI, and human understanding," I said.

"So how hard are these?" Lucia asked.

"Pretty hard for a human and very hard for a robot, as it's not about logic but tricky language understanding," I said, bringing something up on my phone. "For example, the middle one last year was:

It cannot be seen whenever it's there
It fills up a room, it's much like the air.
It cannot be touched, there's nothing to hear
It is quite harmless…

"…there's nothing to fear. Oh, nice, I get it," Li interrupted.

"You knew the answer already?" 10 asked, finally sitting up, brow furrowed.

"Yes," Li said.

Li shuffled over toward 10 and covered her eyes with both hands. "Do you see it now?" Li whispered into 10's ear.

"Ok, ok, hands off," 10 said.

Sigh.

"And finally, please, part three?" Lucia asked.

"Ok, the big finale. **Part three**, the final day, is the physical part. The obstacle course. They tell you the different parts but not the order," I said.

"This year's obstacles are…"

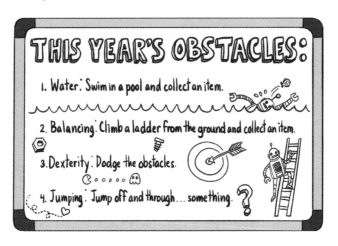

"Plus, there's always a sprint to finish," 10 said, looking back at her screen.

"Yes, sure, a short sprint," I said. "First place gets twenty-five points, second twenty, third fifteen, and anyone who finishes after third gets five. Each year there are about ten teams that enter, although Mrs. D'Silva said there are more this year for some reason."

"Maximum seventy-five points. Here is how last year went," and 10 wrote the scores up on the whiteboard.

	Dalk / Ukko	10 / Ezili
Creative	18	9
Mental	20	15
Physical	25	20
Total	63	44

"I was almost twenty behind Dalk…yup, just twenty points to win. Should be a breeze," 10 said.

"So we break it down." Lucia suggests. "Each of you owns a section but helps one another when needed. AZ, what should everyone look after?" Lucia asked.

"Yes, each has their own section. So, um, how about…no, that won't work, why don't we…"

"What are each of your strengths?" Lucia suggests.

"Well, I'd say, it would make sense for Li to take creative. And 10, you got second in physical last year, and you know, that was pretty good," I said.

"Yes, I came second, but over a minute behind, so it wasn't exactly a photo finish…"

"But better than you did on mental, so you should keep physical. Which leaves mental to me."

"Good. You all own a part and aim to win." Lucia says. "Now all we need is a plan, to execute it, put in the work, and we stand a chance of winning. We also get to play against Dalk's biggest weakness."

"Which is?" I asked.

"His arrogance." Lucia replied. "It's inconceivable to him that he could lose, so we must play to that. The element of surprise."

We all stared at her.

"Well, what did you do last year, 10?" Lucia prompted.

"I had some ideas, spent every waking hour building my robot, did a quick test the day before, and hoped for the best," 10 said.

"Yes, well that's one method. I have another one for building robots, or anything really. I call it a Nine Plan. Here is how it works," Lucia said.

A Nine Plan

1. Set three goals
Begin with the end objective. Write down what you want to achieve and what will have happened for you to have achieved it.

2. Set three steps
How do you get from where you are now to the goal? What three big steps do you need to take? Try working backward from the goals as well as stepping forward until you find a sequence that feels good.

3. Do three tests per week
New technology is about learning. If you only do one test, you only learn one thing and only have one chance to work it out. The more small, fast tests you do, the more chances you have of working it out.

"Goal, plan, test, repeat. How much time do you have left?" Lucia asked.

"The competition starts in eighteen weeks. With school, activities, and other life necessities, you know, like eating, sleeping, the occasional shower…"

"Soccer…" 10 added.

"Meditation…" Li added.

"All those things. We've all said we can do about twenty hours a week, so about 360 hours in total," I said.

"Ok, so with eighteen weeks with three tests per week, you've got fifty-four tests you can perform. Yes, it sounds like a lot, I know, but if you think about them as small tests, it's not so bad. For instance, you've got the physical part, 10, what's one thing you have to solve?" Lucia asked.

"Well, it has to go underwater so it has to be water-resistant at least, preferably waterproof. We have to build it, submerge it..." 10 started.

"Yes, you could build the whole thing and then submerge it, but what if that doesn't work and there's something big we have to change? We might run out of time. How could we do a smaller test, faster? What if I said you have to test it in just twenty-four hours and, if you did, you would get tickets to the next women's soccer World Cup?"

"Twenty-four hours? You can't even build a robot *part* in twenty-four hours! Maybe put something else in it. Just to see if it works. Maybe get an old part?"

"Or not even a robot part. What about an electronic toy?" I said.

"Or a piece of paper?" Li said.

"Yeah, I guess so, anything that would show water got in. You could test that in two hours," 10 said.

"Exactly. We just increased our speed of learning dramatically. We have gone from one lesson in eighteen weeks, which was about four hundred hours of work time, to one test in two hours. That's two hundred times faster," Lucia said.

"Plus us. There are three of us. So, if we are all testing at the same time, we are actually six hundred times faster. *Zoooooooooom*," Li said, with arms out wide like a plane and circling the others.

"Exactly, Li. And a team doesn't just increase speed. It should increase both the quality and creativity of your experiments. Do you see why?" Lucia asked.

"Well, we have different sets of ideas and skills, which can help each other. But I'm not sure they're all so completely different," I said, then looked at Li, who was still flying around us making plane noises, and added, "Though maybe we're overachieving on the creativity side?"

"Yes. And this is important. The only way for the team to maximize speed, quality, and creativity of learning is through tough love," said Lucia. "The tough. You can't just be nice to each other. If someone does something that isn't good enough, not working or not fast enough, you need to tell them. Immediately and clearly." Lucia said.

"This I like," said 10, almost smiling.

"There must also be love, the second part," added Lucia. "Being tough doesn't mean you need to be rude or mean. It has to come from love. It also means you have to help move forward and try again. Every test we learn from is good. Each problem we solve creates momentum. You can't just knock down; you need to help rebuild. Tough and loving. Do you think you can all commit to that?"

"I'll do the love, love, love," said Li.

"It won't work that way," I said. "If we're just tough, we'll all hate it and give up. If we're just loving, we'll be happier, but we won't create anything worthwhile. It has to be both."

"Ooooohhhhhh," hummed Li, eyes sparkling like snow in the sun. "Yes. I am now both loving and tough. Lucia, your garden needs weeding. I'll help. 10, pushing people away is silly, it's making your life less amazing, I will be here when you are ready. AZ, stop doubting yourself. You will be a great leader and you need to start now."

With that, Li got up and walked outside. Lucia flattened her skirt against her lap and lost a battle with a smile. 10's fingers hung frozen above her keyboard.

With my vision blurred, I imagined this was what it felt like to stand at the door of a plane about to parachute for the first time.

This feeling of vertigo stayed with me until the next morning. I woke up and I found the answer. I decided that I was going to take Li's advice and stop doubting myself. I will make mistakes, but a wrong decision is better than no decision. This is the path I will make for myself.

T-Minus Nine

Week One of the New Team Ada—Robot Version 2.0

After school the next day, 10 and Li walked into the lab to find me writing on the whiteboard. 10 sat down at her desk and opened her laptop without saying a word. Li sat down on the ground in front of me. I wondered what impact Li's tough love sharing has had on the team.

"Let's not start with Ada today. Let's set some clear goals," I said. Then, after what felt like an eternity, 10 closed her laptop and spun to face the whiteboard. My heart was racing.

"Write down your goal for your section," I said.

The whiteboard read:

1. Creative-Get perfect scores on all five areas and get 25 points

2. Mental- Get all five answers correct and get 25 points

3. Physical- Come first in the race and get 25 points

"A perfect seventy-five, never ever achieved before. Riiiiight. Someone's going to end up unhappy, probably all of us," 10 said.

"10, be positive, please," Li said.

"This is what we're aiming for. We may get lower, and that's ok. But we are aiming high," I said.

Then each of us went through our parts and, together, we came up with a big list of ideas and challenges. No less than eighteen times,

10 said to herself, not very quietly, "We should be building. We're wasting time…" I ignored her and pushed forward.

The first item for testing by 10 was a new type of actuator for leg thrusters that would help Ada in the jumping section.

> Definition: **Actuator**—A component of a machine that is responsible for controlling and moving.

After two days of work and a slow countdown from four to zero (Li's idea), 10 initiated the actuator. It did nothing until prodded, then spun out of control, and lodged itself directly above Li.

"Next test!" I yelled.

We quickly got into a good rhythm of thinking, building, and testing. Each of us in our own unique way.

Li's work was a mix between a field of flowers and a tornado. One moment Li would be on the ground with poster-sized pieces of paper and charcoal, drawing a dozen variations of some strange pattern. Then, suddenly, Li would stand up, and walk out for ten minutes. Or we could find Li doing yoga, hands on the floor, knees out, balancing for ten minutes in what we were later told was the Bakasana yoga balancing pose.

Li's first test was herself doing the performance Ada would do. It took nine minutes (three times too long), didn't make sense, and almost ended up in a twisted ankle.

"Next test!" I yelled.

I was immersing myself in artificial intelligence, or AI. If Ada was going to be able to answer tricky riddles, I needed to give not just intelligence, but wisdom.

My first test was to see how long it would take to feed the entire internet into Ada and process it. Answer: infinity. By the time you finished processing what was currently on the web, the internet would be eight times larger.

"Next test!" 10 and Li said in chorus.

Week Twelve, Robot Version 3.61

We completed forty-three tests in twelve weeks. Most of them failed, but we learned something from each one.

10 took the lead on assembling all the hardware, though both Li and I were getting a lot better with the tools.

Li led the design and took painstaking care, paying attention to every tiny detail. 10 and I eventually came to see how design isn't just how one piece looks. Design is also how it moves, feels, and interacts with the other parts. This was hammered home when Li suggested adding a curve to the shoulder of Ada that allowed a new range of motion that 10 hadn't achieved before.

I was developing a hard-won love and respect for coding. Each keystroke felt insignificant, but they combined to create something that could do something amazing.

It was hard work. Then more hard work. And then, even more hard work…

Finally, the day came that the 3,491 components and 148,245 lines of code formed the Ada we would come to know and love.

I wanted to remember this moment, so I looked around the room slowly and took a big breath in. It felt alive with possibility and smelled like a toolbox. I looked at Ada's feet on the smooth floor and slowly crept my gaze up. The hard, plastic outer shell looked like deep red copper dipped in oil, with the colors changing with every flicker of light. It had the appearance of constant movement.

Robots aren't people, I knew that, but thousands of years of human nature still drew me to the face of our creation. Li had encouraged a design with strong eyes, to help people feel comfortable communicating, as well as to allow Ada to learn how to show strong empathy.

Instead of two eyes, Ada had eighteen lenses. They could focus in eight directions, process images at 10,000 frames per second, plus record everything for perfect memory.

"Come on, Ada. You are ready," I said.

"I can't watch. But I can't look away," 10 said.

" 'The future belongs to those who believe in the beauty of their dreams.' Thanks, Eleanor Roosevelt," Li said.

I tapped a key and powered up our new friend.

Three slow seconds ticked by.

"Hello, I'm Ada," the robot said, head slowly turning.

"Hello Ada, I'm AZ. It's great to finally meet you," I said.

I took a breath and closed my eyes.

After a few tests, we found that all Ada's systems were functioning. She responded well. And slowly, against all my worries, I started to believe there was something about this version of Ada that was different. Maybe it was because I've put so much of myself into Ada the past few weeks. Maybe it was because we all worked on it together.

Suddenly, my smile melted into a grimace of anguish and fear. Doubt poured in. My hands clenched and opened. I took a deep breath, opened my eyes, and looked Ada in the eyes.

In one way, I've only just met Ada, but really, we've been together for weeks. Can you really feel this way about something you've built? Why is it different this time? This was it. There was no starting again.

I wiped at my cheek, let go of a short, relieved laugh, and gave Ada a hug.

"Thank you," said Ada.

With just eight weeks to go, Lucia suggested we do a practice competition. We weren't totally ready, but it was important to warm up and test early. "The more you practice the final goal, the more prepared you'll be."

Creative Challenge Test

Lucia would judge all five areas, sitting in a chair in the middle of the room with her tablet computer and stylus ready.

"Ok, let's see it," Lucia boomed.

Music filled the air and Ada came to life. It was 180 seconds of pure, average, awkwardness.

Li clapped and cheered. Everyone else was silent.

"AZ, what did you think?" Lucia asked.

"Ok, well, um, it was pretty good—" I said.

"Stop it. Don't be soft. Be tough. Remember: tough love," Li said.

I swallowed, took a breath, and stepped up. "It needs work. It needs oomph. It needs sizzle. It needs something. I see what you're trying to do, but it's not doing it."

"Yes, it does," Li replied.

"I'm no expert in this, but if I had to rate it, this is what my guess would be," Lucia held up her tablet:

- Creativity: 3
- Content: 2

- Movement: 3
- Crowd participation: 3
- Crowd appreciation: 1
- Total: 12 out of 25

Li nodded, bowed, and spun. "The work will be done."

"10, you need to help Li here," I said.

Looking up, pointing to herself, 10 asked, "Me? You saw last year's effort. It's really not my thing."

"Li can do the creative but doesn't know what Ada can do physically. And I want you to aim high. Who is a really athletic, fast soccer player?" I asked.

"Ellie Carpenter. From Australia. Definitely. She is athletic, strong, and she moves like quicksilver. You want me to make Ada move like Ellie? How would *we* do that? How would *we* even think about that?" 10 asked herself. 10 looked up and gave a cheeky, quarter moon smile that I'd never seen before.

Engineers love a challenge.

Mental Challenge Test

"Ada, come and sit here," I said, gesturing to the chair in front of Lucia.

Ada moved over, sat down, and looked at Lucia.

"Here we go," I said. "Three test riddles. One easy, one medium, one hard. Number one…"

> A pal to the earth, though we never meet,
> I have no water but drive the tide,
> When I'm full I can light a street,
> And few have seen my dark side.

"The answer is the moon," Ada said.

"Good start, let's try a harder one. Number two," I said.

I collect water, but I'm not a bucket,
Your imagination can shape me but I'm not clay,
I can be white and fluffy but I'm not a sheep,
If you don't see me, it can be a nice day.

"Yup, up a notch. Game on," 10 said, closing her laptop and watching.

"Clouds," Ada said.

"Wonderful work. That was harder," Li said.

"Number three. The hard one," I said.

Wet or dry,
Low from high,
Runs to die,
On seas nigh.

"How many notches up was that one?" I said, looking over Lucia's shoulder and reading the riddle again.

"Yes, tough. I could answer it but it's better if you work it out for yourself," said Lucia, smiling.

"The fifth question is always really tough. Dalk is the only one who's ever gotten it right, and he doesn't get it every year. I'm with you, that's hard-core. That one's next to impossible," 10 said looking to Ada.

"I don't know the answer," Ada said.

"It's a river," Li said, making us all look over.

"Looks like AZ could do with some of your…" 10 made a motion in the air, "gifts?"

"Yeppity yep. Love to," Li said. "We should also do walking, smelling, and lots of touching of different shapes. Thinking different is only one-ninth of the spectrum," Li said.

Physical Challenge Test

"Ok, let's go," 10 said.

Four stations were set up around the room. The exact sequence and makeup of the obstacle course were never revealed until the day of the competition, so the best we could do was imagine how it was set up and prepare for anything. Ada went through tests for dexterity, balance, and recovery fairly well, but…

"The final test is water. Most years, they have a portable pool that the robots need to jump into and do something. For now, we'll just test Ada's ability to stay underwater for a minute," 10 said.

10 had set up a large tub, half-filled with water. She walked Ada over toward it and gave a last check. "Ok, bath time, please get into the tub and submerge," 10 said.

Ada put a foot into the tub and waited. It looked like Ada was checking for the water temperature. Seconds ticked by.

"The only audible sound is four humans breathing," said Ada, breaking the silence and making us all laugh.

"We're a little tense, Ada, it's been a big day, and these are important tests," I said, hand on Ada's shoulder.

"Each day is 23 hours 56 minutes and 4.1 seconds long. How can a day be 'big'?" Ada asked, putting a foot into the tub and starting to sink down.

"It's not the time ticking by, Ada, it's what you fill your seconds with," Li said.

"I understand," Ada replied.

Ada sank further into the tub and then stopped suddenly.

"Water sensed in upper leg actuator. WATER BREACH CORE. WATER BREACH CORE," Ada said.

We all reacted instantly and uselessly. 10 and I both grabbed for Ada's leg and our heads collided, letting out a synchronized "Owww." Li, after looking left and right, sat down, thumb and pointer finger pinching on both hands and started deep breathing.

"Li, help us, now please," I said, clutching my throbbing head. Li got up quickly. "10, get Ada's feet, Li, hold the left side, I've got the right. Lift up and onto the towel."

With a lot of splashing and a number of shouted direction adjustments, Ada was finally lying down.

"Ada, diagnostics check," 10 shouted.

"Core breached. Major damage. Initiating preventative shutdown mode," Ada responded.

Ada's head tilted back slowly to the ground. The room was silent. 10 started crying.

I looked on hopelessly as Ada's lights went out.

What have I done? We tested the waterproofing, and still it didn't work. Why does everything fail? Why does every failure feel so bad?

10 was still crying, Li looked frozen, and Lucia was staring straight at me.

I'm in this now and there is no turning back.

"Hey, everyone, pull it together. We can do this. It's going to be electrical damage, which can be fixed—"

"We won't have time to fix Ada and make the improvements," 10 said, through her tears.

"We can. We really can! We're a team. Dalk may have resources and deep pockets, but he doesn't want it more than us and he doesn't have a team who cares like us," I said.

I looked into Li's eyes and nodded firmly. Then I sat down with 10, who was looking at Ada with despair.

I know how you feel, 10. We've hurt our friend by not doing a good enough job.

"We owe it to Ada. We have to persist. We have to finish what we started. Let's look after Ada," I said.

10 nodded.

I sat back, breathing fast, not at all sure how we would overcome this challenge but knowing that we must.

T-Minus Eight

D alk sat on a very large, black leather lounge chair, in a very
large office, with his very large father looking out the very large
windows. His father, Jax, sipped coffee from a Jax Robotics coffee cup
and feverishly flicked between two mobile phones and three laptops.
The office was a long rectangle with a door at one short end. When
you entered, you took a long walk past a small table with an odd black
sculpture on it to Jax's desk and very tall chair. The walls reflected the
room on their surface of rough, matte steel.

Dalk looked down at his tablet screen, which showed a black and
white image of AZ, Li, and 10 sitting on the ground with a broken but
otherwise very impressive robot. The image zoomed in on AZ's face.
There was no audio, but it looked like she had just given a speech. Her
body language was trying very hard to say, "I'm not giving up."

But you should, Aye Zed, you should just give up. Please.

Dalk lowered the tablet, cracked his knuckles, and tried yet again
to get his father's attention.

"I checked up on AZ. The robot is the best I've seen but it buzzed
out with a waterproofing test. So it has some major issues. It may
not be ready in time," Dalk said, then waited a minute for a reply
but got nothing from his father but the soft *tap tap* of his fingers on
his phones.

"She is working with two other school friends. The loser I've
beaten for three years in a row and the oddest student in our whole
school," Dalk said, again, into silence. "Oh, and some woman with
silver hair is helping her too."

"What?" Jax's reply came, short and sharp.

"There was an older lady there with the three of them. She was—"

"Older lady? Who? Where? Show me a photo!" Jax put his
phones in separate breast pockets of his black suit jacket.

"Um, just an old lady, um, I don't know, I've never seen her
before." Dalk fumbled for his tablet and held it out.

Jax snatched it from him, manipulated it furiously, and
then froze.

"Lu…cia… Ma…cha…do," Jax said.

Dalk edged back on the lounge chair. He knew what was coming.

"Lucia Machado! LUCIA MACHADO!" Jax, now yelling, dropped the tablet on the ground. "You fool. Do your research. Don't assume. She's a threat. A real one. She's got experience and money. She's bankrolling them. She's trying to get me. She's trying to stop me. Somehow, she must know my plans. You simply must not lose. Fix this!"

Jax then turned his attention to the computer displays on his desk, typing and muttering.

Dalk got up, smoothed his clothes, and fixed his hair. He looked to his father, his mouth open, about to ask something. His father didn't look at him. Dalk picked up his tablet and walked out with the *tap tap tap* of his father's keyboard echoing behind him.

T-Minus Seven

Two weeks later

It was Tuesday afternoon and there were six weeks left before the competition. All teams had to bring their robot to the school hall for a safety check and formally submit their entry form.

10, Li, and I wheeled Ada on a low wagon, covered with an old, blue sheet. We entered the hall which had been cleared of tables and chairs to a low, buzzing murmur. Nearly everyone looked up at us. I held my breath and almost tripped on my own feet. 10 stood up, put her hands in her jean pockets, and glanced back at the door.

"Hi everyone," Li said with three wide hand waves, wonderfully breaking the tension.

You're awesome, Li.

"Come on, team," I said, regaining some composure and pushing the wagon again.

Finding a space in a corner, I looked around the room and saw ten other teams with robots. Some of them looked like hobby projects that would struggle, but most were quite well-developed.

Dalk and his team were the noisiest by far. He had four other people with him: two girls and two boys. They all wore black boots, black jeans, and black jackets with their logo: a black square with a blood-red border, two red eyes and a rectangular red mouth.

There were another five or six people hanging around them, listening to Dalk talking. One of them pointed at us and Dalk turned around. The smile on his face turned into a scowl as he stared right at me. Our plan was to play up to his arrogance, so I feigned panic and quickly looked away. But when I looked back, Dalk was still looking at me and kept adjusting the watch on his wrist.

I've never seen him look like that. Have we really got him so worried? What are you thinking, Dalk?

"Ok, ok, come on now, settle down," Principal Tajek spoke on a microphone in the middle of the hall, waving his arms to encourage quiet. "Ok, ok, welcome everyone, today we're taking entries for this year's robot competition. Ok, now here is Mrs. D'Silva to tell you more."

"Thank you, Principal Tajek. Good morning, students," Mrs. D'Silva said, with a lot more energy and life than the principal, though the reply from the students was the typical slow monotone.

"That's the spirit. This is going to be a big year for the robot competition. We have four more teams than last year, 60 percent of team members are female, and we have at least double the tension already, which is great."

"Today we will just be checking that your robot is basically safe. Also, that it is a robot built by students, and not by, oh, say, a global robotics company."

The hall filled with *oohs* and a few giggles. Dalk pulled out his phone and started typing.

"When we call out your team number, come to the middle of the hall with your robot. Each robot has to have a short conversation, place part of its body in this tub of water and then walk around those five cones. Team One, Huffleclaw, you're up," Mrs. D'Silva yelled into the microphone. "Nice. I like it. Some props given to the 'other' houses in Harry Potter. Could have gone with Ravenpuff, but you probably made the right choice."

There were two members of Huffleclaw, a girl named Katrin and a boy named Matias, who wheeled their robot to the center of the hall. Katrin lifted a small, homemade flag above them of a yellow badger with blue wings.

Their robot was also yellow and blue, about four feet tall, with a pyramid-shaped head, one arm with two joints coming out of the front (or back) and it moved on continuous tracks.

Definition: **Continuous track**, also called tank tread or caterpillar track, is a system of vehicle propulsion in which a continuous band of treads or track plates is driven by two or more wheels.

The school librarian, Mr. Jabari, was with team Huffleclaw in the center of the hall. I watched as the team turned on their robot and Mr. Jabari asked it a few questions from his tablet, looking up and occasionally nodding. The hall was too noisy for me to hear the questions, despite following Li's suggestion to close my eyes.

"Don't worry, technically, this is the easiest part. Total level one. Ada will be fine. Should be," 10 said, head in her laptop.

We were the ninth team in line, so I pretended to do final check-ups on Ada to distract myself but kept watching. Team Huffleclaw easily navigated the five cones and got an exaggerated thumbs-up from Mr. Jabari, and the two team members gave each other a relieved fist bump.

After that came another seven teams. I made notes about all of them in my little green book.

Number	Team name	Description of robot
1	Huffleclaw	Blue and yellow, about sixty cm tall, with a pyramid-shaped head, one arm with two joints coming out of the front (or back) and moved on continuous tracks. Did ok, but not fast.
2	Sharks With Lasers	Blue and silver, low, triangle shape, three arms from the top. Seemed ok but made a lot of odd noises.

| 3 | HAL 45.3 | White, humanoid, lots of red LED lights. Was slow but precise going through the cones. |
| 4 | Tiger | The size of a small tiger with blocky legs and square head, a few orange/yellow and black stripes on its back. When it placed a foot in the tub it gave off a bright blue spark which made a loud noise and a smell like rotten eggs. They were given one week's notice to fix it to be able to enter the competition. |

| 5 | Streaky | Odd shapes, stacked precariously on top of each other with visible wires. Fell over at first cone and caught fire. One-week warning. |
| 6 | Ukko | Dalk's team, Ukko looked like Li described. Nearly two meters tall, jet black, shiny, round head covered in small circles which were lights, sensors and cameras—the head looked alive. Ukko's body looked strong, with all four limbs big and robust. It did the physical test so fast a lot of other teams clapped. Dalk bowed and stared at me again. He is nuts. |

| 7 | Astro Dude | Short humanoid, black feet, spiky head. Moved fast. It was actually pretty good. |
| 8 | Rob Marley | Almost round, a meter diameter, with green paneling and a wig of dreadlocks duct-taped on top. They couldn't seem to get it started, resulting in a big fight between the team and then Mr. Jabari when he gave them the one-week warning notice. |

"Team Nine, Ada," yelled Mrs. D'Silva into the mic.

The whole hall was watching as I walked to the wagon. I took a breath and quickly pulled the blue sheet off. There was a collective gasp as 10 turned Ada on and it started some slow, deliberate movements.

10, Li, and I had tripled our efforts since the failed water test and the focus on teamwork had paid off. We asked each other for help, and it led to better work and a stronger connection.

Li's suggestions for data inputs to help the mental, riddle component seemed odd to me, and completely ludicrous to 10. We went to a market and felt the skin of different fruits. We played the number two top song from every year since 1969 from three different countries. We spent an hour talking about the color yellow. If nothing else, I knew no one else would have done that.

To Li's unbridled joy, 10 had embraced adding some of Ellie Carpenter's grace to Ada. Coming to the lab early one day, I even found Ada with a soccer uniform on doing basic drills.

Following the disaster in the tub, waterproofing became a priority. 10 alternated between defensiveness and denial. Eventually I found that a combination of questions, challenges, and uninterrupted time worked best with 10.

We had also worked, under Li's direction, to make Ada look better. Ada was 165 centimeters tall, a lot shorter than Ukko. Humanoid shape. Arms and legs, lean and curved. Shoulders smaller than a human, with arms starting out at a slight angle, giving the impression of readiness. Strong legs, with knees that allowed for full 360-degree range of motion.

Ada's color was impressive; 10 had even complimented Li. It was a metallic blur of purple, blue, and red. You couldn't tell where one color stopped and another began. On Ada's chest was the team's new logo. It was a hex nut with a heart inside. A blue background to represent the sky and a green heart for nature.

Causing the biggest sensation by far was Ada's waist. Dalk was
the only one who didn't seem impressed, though I think I saw the
tiniest movement on his jawline. Ada's middle section was a steel
gray ball. It allowed Ada's torso and legs to rotate freely. It was a true
innovation and a big risk for the team.

10 had a sketch of it on her wall and in our second week working
together I asked her what it was. 10 got very excited by what it could
do and the difference it would make. 10 didn't really want to, but we
showed Lucia.

Lucia spent almost ten minutes looking at the sketches without
saying anything. We all stood in Lucia's study waiting and taking
in the amazing room. Finally Lucia put the paper down, took her
glasses off, and looked at us. "This design must have two power
supplies, yes?"

"Um, sure, probably," 10 said.

"No, not probably, definitely. We don't have time for probably.
You'll be using magnetic resonance to maintain balance and this will
require a stronger gyrometer," Lucia stated, more than asked.

Definition: **Gyrometer**—A device that looks like a
spinning wheel or disc, used for measuring velocity
and balance.

10 sat up straighter, looked at me and Li, then back to Lucia and said firmly, "Yes, but…"

"You'll need to adjust actuator signaling as well. What will you use for data and communications between the three parts, since you can't hardwire?"

"Low power NFC, but that's easy compared to the machining and the curved circuitry, and I have no idea how to even start on the heat management," 10 said.

Lucia picked up her phone, a model none of us had ever seen before. She said something into her phone, and she turned it toward us as an image of 10's drawing appeared on the screen.

"Call Dasan," she instructed her phone, and a few seconds later a man's voice filled the room.

"Hi Lucia. I'm looking at the sketches you just sent me now… Nice. Who did this? When do you need it done?" said Dasan over the speakers.

"We have six weeks, but this must be support and data only. There is a team of three I'll send to you who must do implementation. Hardware lead is named 10. Dasan, she designed it and she's like you thirty years ago," Lucia said, making 10 blink slowly three times.

"Update in two hours," said Dasan.

"Thanks," Lucia said, as the call ended. Then she turned to me, "You met him in the café and passed his test."

"What test?" I asked.

"He was one of five tests. If you found him and convinced him you were serious and worthy, he'd lead you to me. Now, he's heading to your lab and will meet you in twenty-eight minutes to get to work on this. Don't be late."

"What did you mean I'm 'like Dasan'?" 10 asked.

"When I met Dasan, he was smart and dedicated, but cynical. It's a hard path to get from you to where he is now, but it's a possible and worthwhile one if you choose to walk it. You now have twenty-seven minutes. Go. And 10? This is good work, well done," Lucia said.

10 nodded with a small frown and walked out with us. A few minutes later, as we sat on the bus to meet Dasan, she finally spoke. "For three years I've been beaten. I wasn't good enough, no matter how hard I worked. Ok, I've got some good ideas, but ideas are worthless without action—you've got to make them real. Now we are doing better but in a team. Am I good enough now? Lucia is pretty hard, and she doesn't dish out compliments very often. Maybe I am? That design for the waist is solid. Maybe I shouldn't be so hard on myself?"

"Yes, and yes," said Li, with an arm around 10.

I smiled and enjoyed the moment.

Weeks of hard work later, and the people in the hall were mesmerized by Ada and the innovative waist.

"They can say ooh and ahh as much as they like but until it actually works, it's just shiny vaporware," 10 said. "Ok, let's get through this checkpoint and get back to work."

Definition: **Vaporware**—Software or hardware that has been advertised but is not yet available to buy, either because it is only a concept or because it is still being written or designed.

Li was completely fine with accepting the praise, bowing like a circus master.

After 10 made a few keystrokes, the light in Ada's eyes flashed on. We helped Ada off the wagon.

"Ready, Ada?" I said.

"Yes, let's do this," Ada replied with a fist pump and a full waist spin, getting the crowd *oohing* again. Ada stepped off the wagon and together we walked over to take the tests.

We'd answered thousands of harder questions than what would be asked in the competition, we had water tested a dozen times, and the cones were barely a warm-up for what 10 had Ada doing these days. This should be a breeze.

Ada passed the first test very easily. Before the water test, 10 was sweating and massaging her forehead, but there were no errors. 10 even smiled.

Ada then lined up for the cones test and I looked over toward Dalk, who was watching intently, his tablet in both hands.

He must be videoing Ada. Ha, at least he's taking us seriously.

"Go!" Mr. Jabari said.

Ada took off. Around the first cone, then the second and third with grace. Approaching the last cone, clearly very fast, Ada lost balance and was about to fall. Ada's waist twisted to adjust the center of gravity, leaned deep into the corner, and just made it. The crowd's gasps turned to wild cheers.

That looked cool. Ok, now slow down.

Ada was supposed to stop within five meters of the cone, but instead, sped up.

Oh no, something is going wrong. Do something about it. But what?

"10, Ada's going too fast. Stop her," I yelled.

10 typed furiously.

"Ada, stop. Ada, emergency shutdown. Abort. Abort. Abort," I yelled.

As the crowd realized something was wrong, waving hands covered mouths and cheers turned to gasps.

It happened very fast. Faster than I could think.

Ada was heading toward the closed exit door, between the teams Huffleclaw and Rob Marley. I was confident that the robot laws would kick in and, if it came to it, Ada would run into the closed door and avoid harming anyone.

The Three Laws of Robotics

1. A robot may not injure a human being or, through inaction, allow a human being to come to harm.
2. A robot must obey orders given to it by human beings except where such orders would conflict with the First Law.
3. A robot must protect its own existence as long as such protection does not conflict with the First or Second Law.

I started walking toward Ada. I could see the communication LEDs around Ada's neck blinking out of control.

What are you doing, Ada? Why won't you stop? And why aren't I running? Why won't my legs listen to me?

Then, to my horror, Ada changed course and headed directly toward Katrin and Matias from Huffleclaw. They were still stuck to the spot in fear. Luckily, their instincts had them jump quickly away and hide behind their robot.

"ABORT. OVERRIDE. ABORT. OVERI—" Ada's voice echoed throughout the room until the impact.

Ada crashed full speed into Huffleclaw. The noise was like metallic thunder. The robots, in a tangled mess of metal and wires, collided with Katrin and Matias. The four of them—two haywire robots and two helpless humans—smashed into the wall behind them.

T-Minus Six

The room exploded into chaos. Screams, feet running, and me yelling, "Noooooo!" I'd finally broken out of my shock and started to run toward the mess, trailing behind 10.

"Please, everyone, remain calm. Move to the exits," Mrs. D'Silva called out over the microphone. People ran for their lives.

10 got to the accident before anyone else. She roughly pulled Ada's broken body off the top of the awful pile. Mr. Jabari arrived next and with 10, they tore Huffleclaw away from the bodies. Katrin's eyes were open, though she had several gashes on her forehead and her chin. She held her arm up limply and was breathing in shallow gasps.

"Oh my," said Mr. Jabari.

Matias was lying on the floor with his leg at an odd angle. His eyes were closed but he was breathing.

I arrived and I put both shaking hands to my face. I could smell the acrid burning of electronics and the rusty, full smell of blood. I knelt down and took Ada's head in my hands.

Ada looked up and said quietly, "I'm...sorry..."

"Oh Ada, this can't have been your fault. You would *not* do this..." I said disbelievingly, wracking my brain for answers.

Looking at every detail of Ada's face, I felt the soft vibration of the still-operating internal motors slowly stop still.

Li, Mrs. D'Silva, and a handful of other students formed a circle around the area.

10 took off one of her shoes and used a sock to tie around Katrin's arm to apply pressure to the wound and stem the bleeding.

"I've called for ambulances," Mrs. D'Silva said.

Mr. Jabari gently pulled Matias away from the wall and lay him down. He put his fingers on his neck and three slow seconds passed. "He's alive, but unconscious." Sighs rippled through the gathered group.

"AZ, 10, Li, leave your robot. To my office," Mr. Tajek said.

I didn't move, holding Ada's hand.

"Now!" said Mr. Tajek.

I pulled my eyes away from Ada and we walked from the hall. Sirens filled the empty corridors.

"What just happened?" 10 asked, when the door closed to the principal's office and we were alone.

"It's horrible…we nearly killed two kids…" I said.

"That was the most awful thing I've ever done. I can't go on with this. What did we do?" Li said, walking to the window and looking up to the sky for answers.

"We must've messed something up. But what? How? The testing all passed. Ada, like all robots, has direct and backup coding to make sure they can't harm humans," 10 said.

"All the love. All the goodness we shared with Ada. This is a darkness," Li said.

"Maybe it wasn't us?" I said.

"What? What do you mean? Who?" 10 yelled.

"Well, Dalk had his tablet pointed at Ada. I thought he was filming it. But maybe he did something," I replied.

"Are you serious? Why didn't you say something? Why didn't you do something? Anything? You could have stopped it!" 10 exclaimed.

"It happened so fast. It really looked like he was just videoing it, which isn't strange. And how could I have known this was going to happen? I really didn't know. Please believe me," I pleaded.

"Maybe it wasn't him. How can we tell? How could he do something anyway?" Li asked, still looking at the sky.

"How could he have hacked into Ada? We have strong security. And overriding the base laws of robotics is a big call. I'm not sure Dalk is capable of that, either technically or ethically, not by himself," 10 said loudly, a look of complete disappointment on her face.

The door flung open and the usually reserved Principal Tajek was fuming, with Mrs. D'Silva and Mr. Jabari trailing behind. "What just happened? What did you do? You better have some answers for me. Do you understand how much trouble you're in?"

I tried to get a word in between questions. "We don't know, we'll have to check the data from Ada to find out."

"From who? Who's Ada?"

"Ada is our robot," Li said with clear, cool strength.

"A student, a real person, is very badly injured. Your robot not only lost control but it looked very much like it chose to harm humans rather than harm itself. I don't know a lot about robots, but I know the three laws," Principal Tajek said, finally sitting, putting his head in his hands. "This could bankrupt the school."

"We actually think Dalk might have—" I said.

"Oh no, don't even try…don't even go there…don't try and pass the blame onto someone else," Principal Tajek said with sudden urgency. "You're the team. It's your robot. It's your fault."

The three of us shared looks and were about to try and reply all at once.

"You are all expelled from this school," Principal Tajek said.

Li let out a quick laugh and 10 blocked her ears.

I looked at them both.

This is on me.

"You're right, this is our fault. Or actually, my fault," I said. "I am the one who wrote the safety code. I am the one who should have triple-checked the standard robotics laws were in place. I am the leader of this team and Li and 10 both worked on other parts. I am the one who should be expelled."

10 and Li both went to speak but I gave them both a look that stopped them.

Principal Tajek scanned our three faces.

"Ok, the other two are suspended for a week. And you, as of this moment, you are expelled from this school. Now get out of my sight," Principal Tajek said, picking up his phone and barking instructions to Mrs. D'Silva and Mr. Jabari.

Li, 10, and I walked out of the office and into the corridor. The school was still evacuated and eerily empty. The air was dry, still, and almost bitter. The muffled sound of a siren wailed in the distance.

"Why did you do that?" said 10, breaking the silence.

"I had to. I had no choice," I replied.

"Why didn't you say what Dalk did? Surely it was him. And you flat-out lied. You *did* triple check. We did have the three laws built in," 10 said.

"You heard Tajek. He needs Jax so he can't even think about implicating Dalk. He's crazy angry and I understand why. There is no way he'd listen to us right now," I said.

"But why did you take all of the blame? We are a team. You upset me, AZ," Li said.

"I know. I know. I'm sorry. But I had to. Because I need to ask you to do something for me. Two things really. Can you help me?" I asked.

"Of course. We are a team," Li said.

"Definitely," 10 concurred.

"Ok. Thank you both. Now, please let me explain. We can't all be expelled because you both need to find the evidence to clear this up," I said, with Li and 10 both nodding. "And you'll need access to the school resources to rebuild Ada."

"What? How can that be important right now? And I doubt anyone is going to want to see Ada around," 10 said.

"Because firstly, Ada is a part of our team. Ada is not just a robot. Ada is us and we are Ada," I said, and they both agreed. "Secondly, because we'll need Ada well and functioning to work out how the hack was done for evidence."

10 massaged her forehead gently, then roughly. "Ok, yes, I can do that," 10 said.

"And finally, we need to get Ada back up to full strength for the competition," I said.

"Whoa! You still want to enter? You saw Ada. We'll be lucky to get the data out," 10 said.

"AZ, maybe we should let this go," Li said, with a hand on my arm.

Maybe they're right. But I don't think so.

I paused, took three breaths, and spoke in a slow, calm voice. "Now, more than ever, this team must go on. We may not win the final competition, but if we aren't there, then Dalk and people like him have won much more. They would have beaten our spirit and defeated our right to participate. We owe it to Ada, and we owe it to ourselves," I said.

"You are right, AZ. We can't give up now," Li said through a smile.

"I'm all for trying and I would love to see Ada walk in the door and see Dalk's face drop, but technically we have no way to get everything we need done. We'd need a bunch of people we don't have," 10 said.

"We don't need a bunch. We need a team. And I think I know how to build one," I said. "Here is what we need to do."

T-Minus Five

Two days later, 10, Li, Lucia, and I were working in 10's lab. Ada was lying on a table, still significantly damaged. Lucia was in front of the whiteboard, with two lines creating three big areas marked "backlog," "in progress," and "done." The first area was over half-filled with sticky notes with different things on them.

"Retesting gait, left elbow replace actuator, full rescan of sensors, patch up the waist sphere," 10 said, lying on the ground, looking at the roof with her hands covering her face.

"Ok, slow down a bit…" said Lucia, writing each of the things 10 listed on a separate sticky note and sticking them into backlog. 10 kept listing them until the whole area was completely full. Lucia stood back, took off her glasses and tapped them against her chin.

Li was humming odd tunes, a little more loudly than normal, and writing another letter to her grandmother.

Backlog	In progress	Done
96 tasks	0 tasks	0 tasks

"Ok, what are we looking at?" 10 asked. She sat up, looked at the board and flopped back down again. "Arrrr. Technically, we're toast. Technically, it's impossible. Technically…"

"Technically, we don't know what we can do until we get up and try," I said.

"Weeellll, technically, you might be right, but…" 10 stood up with a groan. "Look at this board. Look at this work. It would take six weeks for us to get this done. We just don't have the resources."

There was a firm, three-beat knock and everyone turned their heads. I ran to the door and opened it quickly. Standing there was Dasan.

"Nice to see you too," Dasan said as my smile turned to a frown. I wasn't expecting him.

"I've asked him to come and help us coordinate," Lucia said.

"Good morning, everyone," Dasan said, walking in holding a large aluminum mug of coffee.

"Great, more 'help,' but you two can't actually do any of the work or we're disqualified and I'm not cheating," 10 said.

"We're not going to cheat, 10. 'Nothing good is ever created by cheating, Li' says my grandmother," Li said.

"No, we're not. That's not us. Not how we do things," I said to the room. 10 nodded.

Dasan looked at the whiteboard, sipped his coffee, looked at the team, sipped his coffee, looked at Ada and sipped his coffee. "Looks like about six weeks of work. How long do we have?"

"Five days to pass the redo of the basic test and then another week after that for the competition," I replied without flinching. "Let's put all things we need to do before we take the basic test at the top and the other ones that can wait to the second week below." I started rearranging the sticky notes.

"Why bother? There is no way—" 10 started.

There was another knock. I walked toward the door, took a deep breath, and opened it. Standing there were five teenagers.

"Hi, thank you so much for coming. Please come in," I said, and the five stepped into the room.

Some of the group gave awkward gestures of greetings. 10 and Li stood still with confused looks on their faces.

"Everyone, I'd like you to meet some people I'd like to join our team. Team Streaky, can you introduce yourselves? Tell us about yourselves and what you like working on," I said.

"Oh, hey, I'm Kora, I live with my three sisters and my mother who runs an accounting company. I like mashed potatoes on toast and I won't be happy if we make the same mistake twice. Oh, and I'm a full-stack programmer," Kora said with more confidence than I had expected. Kora was curvy with a kind face.

> Definition: **Full-stack programmer**—A web developer
> or engineer who can build all parts of a website or
> program, including the front end (what people see) and
> back end (what people don't see).

"Hello, I'm Jerel, I drink a lot of black tea…my mother is a pilot, my dad is a nurse, and I'm easily distracted…I'm a hardware guy… I'm getting into AI," said Jerel with a few awkward pauses matching his awkward hand gestures.

"Ahh, didn't your robot catch fire at the tests?" 10 asked, face contorted.

"Hey, we are the last people who can point fingers," I said, and quickly moved on. "We also have the team that worked on Rob Marley."

"Hey, I'm Maureen. I love communications and security, and I, umm, have a step brother, my mother and dad run the pizza place near the train station, and I guess, umm, yeah, I love music too," she said, while putting her long, dark hair into two pigtails and looking completely relaxed.

"Hello everyone. I'm Adewale," said a voice, stepping out from behind Maureen.

"Can you tell us a bit about yourself?" Li asked.

"Oh, yes. I live with my two sisters and brother, my mother is a doctor, and my dad looks after us kids and paints. I play Dungeons and Dragons, am sensitive about my height, and am obsessed with databases," Adewale said. It's true that he wasn't very tall, but not really short either.

"Hey, hi there. I'm Balanda. I'm the oldest of four kids, my mother is an architect, and my dad is a kindergarten teacher. I think TV is stupid, I go swimming every day in the river by my house, and I'm a hardware tinkerer. I don't like talking about myself," Balanda said with a grimace and sat down quickly. She had light-colored hair, was wiry, and looked very unsure of her decision to join the team.

Ten seconds of silence ebbed by as all these eyes tried to make sense of this new situation. What a wonderfully diverse team.

"Both of these teams have agreed to join with us, and we need it. Just look at that board and all that work to do. We need help. Even with help it's going to be hard, but we can do it, if, right here, right now, we all forget about anything that has come before and just get to work as a team."

I looked at 10 and Li. It was a risky move to bring them in without checking first, but I needed to be bold. Li was of course smiling, nodding, and holding back from dancing. 10 was not impressed. She looked at me, looked at the roof and gave what had to be an intentionally huge sigh. I gulped down some air and pushed on.

"New crew, please meet your team members. This is 10, leading on hardware. Li, leading on creative. Plus our two mentors, Lucia and Dasan. As we all know, the mentors can't do any of the work, but they can help us decide what we do and how we do it. If anyone has any questions, please ask now. And if you're not up for the work as a part of this team, now is the time to go," I said, trying not to show that my hands were shaking.

10 stood up and looked at the new crew of people, the whiteboard, then back to the team. "This is pretty crazy."

"But, technically..." I said.

10 smiled. "Ok, yes, technically, if we can all do our jobs really well, then, yes, technically, we might just make it. So how good are you all?"

The new team members looked around, waiting for someone to speak.

"Well, for starters, there is data being secretly transmitted from this lab...video data... A lot of it," Maureen said.

10 pulled her head back in surprise.

"Video data? Really?" I asked.

"Really? Did you say you do security tech?" 10 said.

"Yeah, I'm sure," Maureen said, looking at her phone. "I can track packets of data being transferred in and out, and there is a fair bit going out that's not through your main router. There's probably a camera somewhere with a wireless chip."

Everyone started looking around on the walls. In the top corner, just near the door, there were two boxes, one of which looked like a smoke detector, the second of which was shiny and black.

"Wait. Everyone stop and look at me," I said loudly and suddenly. "Don't look around. Maureen, is it video and audio or just video?"

"Looks like just video," Maureen said.

"AZ, what's going on?" Li asked.

"I'm not 100 percent sure, but my guess is that Dalk has been watching us. It's why he wasn't surprised by Ada at the pre-competition test. He'd already seen it all. But if it's not audio, then I've got an idea. Everyone follow me."

We walked outside and sat on the grass in a nearby park.

"I think Dalk is using video to spy on us and it probably also helped him hack into Ada. I don't have proof yet, but I think I know how to get it. In the meantime, I say we mess with Dalk's head."

"10, if we use a professional lab, is that allowed?" I asked.

"Yes, it's fine, as long as students do the work," 10 said.

"Great. Dasan, could we use your lab?" I asked.

"Yes, I don't see why not," Dasan said.

"Ok, great. So we move out of our lab, Dalk can't watch us anymore and maybe thinks we've given up. Then he won't try to sabotage us again and we've got the element of surprise. Yeah?" I asked.

"I like it. I'm in," Li said.

"Ok, let's do it. If Dalk did this, then I want Ada back to full health and in that competition," 10 said.

"Everyone else up for this?" I asked and received a collective "yeah" and head nods from the group.

"Ok, game on."

So, with some pretty bad acting, the group pointed to the board, waved their arms about, pretended to have an argument, walked out, and then let fly with some held-in laughter as soon as they were off-camera. 10 was left alone to pack up Ada and key parts into tubs and move them out.

An hour later, 10 arrived at Dasan's lab, where everyone else was working. Balanda had taken a photo of the whiteboard and copied every single task over. She'd also broken them down into those things that needed to get done before the rerun of the pre-test.

"Well, we've found our super-organized person," I said, looking through all the tasks in the project management tool.

Kora had set up a development environment and Jerel, Maureen, and Dasan were talking about hardware issues and what they'd work on first.

"Whoa!" 10 said, much louder than I think she had intended, looking around the lab for the first time. "This is awesome. Impressive tools, Dasan. Look at this stuff. You've got four Roland ARM-1,000 Desktop 3D printers, two Sherline 8TX Series TTP-Ready lathes and two Roland JX-3Z milling machines. All you need is a wind tunnel for aerodynamics."

> Definition: **Wind tunnels**—Large tube-like spaces where air blows through. They are used by organizations like NASA to test how air and space craft models fly.

"Well, we can't expect everything," I said, smiling. "Why don't you put some of those tubs in the storage room through that door?"

10 opened the door, looked in, and fell to her knees. The room erupted in laughter. "Are you kidding me? A wind tunnel? Technically, this is the happiest moment of my life. How come you never showed us this before?"

"You never asked," Lucia said, slightly smirking.

10 stood up and walked to the new whiteboard and looked at the work to do. Li and I joined her. Several of the sticky notes had been put in the "in progress" area in the middle of the board. 10 adjusted a few of the tasks from pre-test to final competition. The new team members were working away alone, or with Lucia and Dasan showing them how to use the equipment.

	Backlog	In progress	Done
Pre-test phase: 4 days	38 tasks	4 tasks	0 tasks
Final competition phase: 10 days	54 tasks	0 tasks	0 tasks

"What do you think, 10? Can we do it?" I asked.

"We can do it, oh, yes we can, we can do it, come on, 10," Li softly chanted.

"With this equipment…if this team is good…if we do little else other than school, work, eat, and some sleep. Technically…it's still unlikely, but just fractionally possible," 10 said, picking up her toolbox. "Let's get to work."

Li and I both sandwich-hugged 10 from either side.

"Ok, ok, enough, let's not get carried away. We're a long way from a happy place," 10 said, eventually smiling.

"As you said, let's get to work. Don't forget to constantly be testing," I said to everyone. "Li, I need your help to get me un-expelled. Adewale is tracing the data to find the source, but he says it's probably obfuscated."

> Definition: **Obfuscate**—To render obscure, unclear, or unintelligible.

"At least it will suggest that we were sabotaged, but we will need more evidence to clear me," I said. "I'm going to try to do what Lucia suggested, play to Dalk's arrogance."

Li: Hey Dalk, it's Li, with Ada out of action, I am looking to join a new team for the robot competition. Can we please meet at La Dolce Vita Cafe today at three thirty to talk more about it?

Dalk: LOL. Ok.

Li was sitting in a booth waiting for Dalk when he walked in at 3:45.

"So what is this really about?" Dalk asked. "You don't strike me as someone who is so madly into robots that you really want a new team and I don't need anyone, certainly not someone like you, so…"

"I've quite enjoyed this new journey of roboticismness. Your robot is wonderful, and I would like to learn more," Li said. "You're clearly much smarter than AZ and 10, given how you were able to hack Ada without them even knowing."

Dalk reached over and grabbed Li's bag and pulled out Li's phone. Li grabbed for it, but Dalk pulled it further away.

"Trying to record a confession?" Dalk laughed aloud. "Come on. Really? That was your attempt to 'get me'? You're pathetic."

Li's eyes narrowed slightly.

"And, if I'm not mistaken…" Dalk said, standing up and walking to the booth behind Li and looking straight at me. I was sitting under the next booth table with my phone recording.

"Ohh, a double-trick. So clever. You nearly got me." Dalk laughed even louder. "Come and join us, AZ."

I crawled out from under the table and sat next to Li, a look of abject dejection on my face.

"Look at you two. So sad. Was that your big plan? I find Li's phone, then I give you a full confession, with AZ recording it in the booth behind. I'm actually surprised you came up with something at least a little interesting. But, unsurprisingly, I'm smarter and you failed. And now, the recording devices are off and it's your low-grade word against my first-class word, and I'm not the tiniest bit scared. So, I'll tell you; I did it, I hacked your robot."

I used every ounce of will to keep a straight face.

"Now, I didn't expect it to crash into people and do so much damage. That's your fault for somehow making it fast. I merely wanted to take it out of action and another robot along with it. The two humans…collateral damage," Dalk said. "But your robot, your blight on the world of robotics, with its gimmicky marble-middle, built by a team of losers… You don't deserve to line up next to me and my glorious warrior."

"Warrior? It's just a friendly competition, Dalk," I said.

"And that's why you'll always lose," Dalk said. "It's so much more than that. If you could only see the vision. But I can't stay here with you lowlifes. I've got a competition to win. I hope you come along to watch me hold the trophy up."

"We'll be there," I said. Li grabbed my hand, which I squeezed and moved it away gently. "We will be there and so will Ada, in the competition, beating you."

Li's head shook from side to side.

"Really? You're going to try and fix that freak? Found another lab, have you? Interesting. You'll never learn, will you?" He stood up and walked off.

"Why did you tell him?" Li asked. "We've lost some of our advantage."

"I know, I'm sorry. I changed my mind and trusted my gut. Hearing him bragging made me realize that with us out that takes the pressure off him. He will find it much harder to put a camera in the new lab and much harder to hack us with our stronger team. I want him wasting his time fretting over us. Plus, he'd find out at the retest anyway, so the advantage would be short lived," I replied.

"Oh AZ, you are getting craftier, but don't we need every advantage we can get? Especially since he is prepared to fight dirty, and we are not," Li said.

"I don't think so. We are just hitting our stride while he is worried. Did you see how he mentioned how fast Ada was? He's actually worried. He said he's not scared, but I think he's bluffing. Otherwise why bother hacking us? And what he doesn't know is that by taking out both Ada and Huffleclaw, he's made our team bigger and stronger. And we may not be playing dirty, but we are certainly getting tougher. I mean, look at your face. You've got your game face on."

Li's face launched into a series of contortions and twitches, finally settling back into its usual smile.

Marveling at my new friend, I picked up the rectangular box that the salt and pepper shakers were sitting on. It looked like fairly plain silver metal, with a few lines on the largest flat side.

"Now Dalk. A double bluff, you say. How about a triple? Did your big brain see the triple coming? No? Apparently not," I said with a serious look on my face, then cracked up in laughter with Li.

I slid the top off the device, exposing some buttons and a small red light. I pressed a few buttons, a green light came on, and Dalk's voice rang out: "…and I'm not the tiniest bit scared. So, I'll tell you—I did it, I hacked your robot…"

The next morning, I'd played the recording for the principal. An hour later, after some frantic phone calls, too many people crammed into Principal Tajek's office. Li, 10, Dalk, and I sat in chairs in front of the desk. On the right side was my mom on her phone and my dad looking very uncomfortable.

Next to them was Li's mother, in active wear like she'd just come from the gym, and Li's dad, in an expensive suit. I'd only met them a few times, but they were lovely and adored Li.

On the other side of my parents was 10's mother in a pair of overalls covered in paint. She was a single mother with an amazing work ethic.

Jax, Dalk's father, stood on the left side and had brought one of his lawyers, "Mister Stone," along with him.

I played the recording again.

"That could be fake. It could have been coerced. It is not an admission of guilt," Mr. Stone rattled off.

"Enough, Stone," Jax interrupted. "This is a waste of my time. It doesn't matter. Tajek isn't going to do anything to Dalk. If he so much as thinks about suspending him for these nothings, I'll have Dalk in another school, along with all my funding, in an hour. We're done here."

Jax walked out, Stone followed, and Dalk, giving us a satisfied look, trailed behind them.

"Are you really going to let them get away with that? They sabotaged us and hurt people. Why isn't he expelled or at least suspended?" 10 asked, a look of disbelief on her face.

"Well, ok, you see, as the man in the suit said, this evidence is interesting, but really, um, does it really prove anything?" Principal Tajek started.

"It proves a lot," my mother said, with a conviction that I'd never seen before. "What about the video data, too? It was premeditated. At the very least, these three are innocent and we should un-suspend them, un-expel AZ, and let them back into the competition."

"Well, there probably isn't much harm in it. Ok, ok, so, that is done, no suspension, no expulsion, back in the competition. But, please, no more drama? Ok? Please?" said Principal Tajek.

"I promise. No drama," I said, hand on my heart.

The next day we're back at the lab working. There was a knock at the door and Li opened it to find Katrin standing there, her plaster cast in a sling, a large graze on her forehead, and a few stitches on her chin. The activity in the room instantly stopped. Li stepped forward to hug her.

"Hey, careful with my arm please," Katrin said, pulling back and allowing a gentle, half-hug from Li. "I'm still a bit tender."

"Hi Katrin, are you ok? How is Matias doing?" I asked.

"Um, he's better and the doctors say he'll probably be ok," Katrin said. "Wow, you have some amazing equipment here."

I noticed everyone still looking at Katrin. "Hey everyone, let's get back to it. We still have a lot to do." I stepped through the door and closed it behind her as the activity ramped up again.

"I'm so sorry about what happened. It was just awful," I said.

"Yeah, it was all awful, but I heard about how Dalk hacked Ada. I was wondering if I could join the team."

I'm literally going to cry. Ok, I am crying.

"Wow, of course. That would be great. We need all the help we can get. Are you sure you're ok to do that?

"I want to keep busy. I sit still too long…and I don't want to give up. Because of Matias being injured too. I don't want that to be the end. I'm not sure what I can do. Do you think I can help you rebuild Ada?"

"Of course, we'd love to have you. And don't worry about the arm, I'm sure we can work something out."

Four days later, the whole team, along with Lucia and Dasan, stood in a circle holding hands. Ada had just passed the second chance pre-competition test and I was doing my favorite "pinky fingers in the air" dance.

The whiteboard looked like this:

	Backlog	In progress	Done
Pre-test: 0 days to go	0 tasks	0 tasks	42 tasks
Final competition: 10 days to go	31 tasks	11 tasks	16 tasks

"Let's get to work," said my voice, which was a bit odd since I hadn't said it. Everyone looked around. Ada had played a recording of my voice. The whole room erupted in laughter.

Ten days of hard work, long hours, not much sleep, a number of small bugs, and a few big ones, later, and the team was finally happy that Ada was ready. All tasks had been completed and Ada had done dozens of tests.

It was ten o'clock the night before the first day of competition. Lucia had bought pizza and ice cream to celebrate. I stood in front of the team, my arm around Ada.

This is getting easier, but why does my stomach start 'pretzeling' every time I stand in front of them?

"What we have done, in the last few weeks, is nothing short of incredible. To see a team with a lot of new members be able to focus, collaborate, and execute was a thrill. Thank you for letting me be a part of it. I'm very proud of what you have done and regardless of the outcome in the next three days, you should know that we have achieved something special. Ada, I want to make sure you know how much you are a part of this team," I gave Ada a hug as some LED lights discoed across the ceiling. "I also want to thank Mrs. D'Silva, Mr. Jabari, Lucia, and Dasan; you've been amazing supporting us and we couldn't have done it without you."

"Or the wind tunnel," 10 added, bringing a few laughs from the group.

"We should all get some sleep. Tomorrow is going to be a big day," I said.

That night, I dreamt I was stuck in a box, operating on Ada with one arm tied behind my back.

T-Minus Four

School Robot Competition
Day One, Part One: Creative

9:45 a.m.
Fifteen minutes to start of competition

I looked around the hall full of activity and felt the energy. Teams were making final touches to their robots. The big crowd waved signs to support their electronic champions.

A small stage sat at one end. There were no special stage lights. No microphones. No instruments. The robots need to bring it all, in more ways than one.

The creative section judges sat at a big table with three chairs in front of the stage. They were Mrs. Tanaka, the local university's design professor, Kajal Qadir, who ran the local dance company, and Ashan Tengku, a famous singer.

Ada was surrounded by the team, generally fussing and carrying laptops, diagnostics equipment, and phones with apps.

"Good morning everyone, we're done, we're good, we're ready. Ada is ready," I said, arms waving to get the team's attention. "Only 10, Li, and I are allowed down here on the floor for the performances, everyone else, big hugs and get up into the grandstands to support us."

"Thank you. No more testing please. Fresh circuits are needed," Ada said.

"Ada, Li, 10, good luck today," I said, holding their hands.

"I am ready," Ada said.

"I'm on a swing, swinging high, about to reach the very top and now...WHOOOOOSSSSSSHHHH," Li said, spinning around.

"Ok, technically I'm very nervous. If we have a bad score here, it's going to be very hard to recover," 10 said, sitting down, then standing up, then kneeling, then standing up again.

"10, you need to do twenty push-ups," Ada suggested, making 10 laugh. "Push-ups will aid in muscle tension release." So 10 did thirty-two push-ups, just to be sure.

I looked over at Dalk and found him staring back at me. He swung his head down and away like he was caught doing something he shouldn't.

"Ok, ok, settle down," said Principal Tajek into the microphone, speaker feedback squealing in everyone's ears. "Please make sure all your core team members are all present, otherwise you can't participate. We have randomly assigned an order. If I call your team name, please bring your robot to the stage and get started. Up first... Astro Dude..."

The crowd cheered as Astro Dude came up to the stage and kicked off the day with a magic show and some jokes about being a robot. It was pretty impressive, and I started to get worried that it wasn't just Ukko we had to beat. The judges' score was 18 out of 25.

After that was:

- **Ozone**—Ozone was android shape, big, bulky, and soft pink. For creative, Ozone sang while dancing. It was pretty clunky. 11 points.

- **Tiger**—narrated and mimed a battle with itself, tumbling, jumping, rolling, spinning. It was very fast and nimble, though confusing at times. 17 points.

- **Shark With Lasers**—was well-named, as it had a laser display telling the story of a baby shark facing the reality that it is a carnivore. The robot used a chant which the crowd joined in on, scoring extra points. 20 points.

- **Deckard**—another robot the team hadn't seen yet. Android shape, two meters tall, very lean, wiry. Deckard did an odd combination of Italian opera and Irish dancing, but it was quite agile, and the crowd appreciated the creativity. 19 points.

Up next was Ukko. There were a few cheers but mostly boos from the audience. Dalk's blame for Ada's accident at the pre-test was meant to be completely private, so obviously everyone knew about it.

Ukko stood in the middle of the stage, facing backward, when an enormous boom rocked the room. It felt like an explosion and some people blocked their ears. The boom continued as Ukko started dancing to the beat.

"That thing must be 50 percent speakers!" yelled 10 over the noise.

"Less room for brains," Ada said, teasing a grin from Li.

Ukko started singing a rock song about winning a race and the crowd actually started clapping along. The dance moves were pretty good, too, and Li was nodding with respect.

Ukko finished with an echoing boom and though a few people crossed their arms in protest, a solid cheer burst from the crowd.

Ukko got twenty-three points.

"Twenty-three? That's huge. That's not good, not good, not good at all," 10 said, massaging her forehead.

"Need to do more push-ups?" Li asked her.

"Ada," called Principal Tajek over the microphone, and I closed my eyes.

So much has led up to this moment. What if I could go back to that classroom so long ago, keep my mouth closed, and let the moment pass? Then I wouldn't have Ada, Li, 10, Lucia, and all the others in my life. But I also wouldn't be petrified.

I opened my eyes and hugged Ada.

"Good luck, you can do it," I said, trying to sound convincing.

"I will break a leg," Ada said.

"What? Why would you say that?" 10 said.

"It's an expression, 10, one of hundreds I taught her," Li said, high-fiving with Ada.

Ada climbed onto the stage and sat cross-legged in the starting position and we walked back to our station. My heart raced and my stomach flipped.

"Ada, initiate creative performance," said 10, checking her laptop.

Ada leaned forward and started tapping on the stage, creating a slow beat. The tapping became a drumming and the noise filled the hall. It suddenly stopped as Ada's hands pressed to the stage, and Ada's legs flipped up into a handstand. Ada then spun on one hand, falling gracefully into a superhero landing—one knee bent to the ground, one fist on the ground. Ada waited, perfectly still, for a second as the crowd *oohed*.

Then Ada stood up with a torso exploding into light, like a mirror ball alive with a crisp image of short video clips. One moment the pyramids, then a polar bear, an accelerated peeling of a carrot, then a person smiling, frowning, smiling.

While this was happening, Ada started B-botting, which is when a robot breakdances. Ada spun on one hand, body off the ground, then left shoulder, right shoulder…it was fast and graceful.

To the crowd's bewilderment, Ada also starting rapping:

> My body is made of wires and chips,
> Instead of blood, I flow bits,
> Pulsing through 500 GIPS,
> I've got some skills, got some wits.
> No daddy, no mommy, so sad,
> I've got family, yeah they're mad,
> They used their hands and what they had...
> Didn't need help from their rich dad.

Some gasps, laughs, and cheers rose from the audience. I saw Dalk and his team sneering and shaking their heads.

Ada was still dancing with acrobatic precision, torso playing a video of hands clapping, and the crowd joined in.

> No nerves, but I've got circuitry,
> My data is my memory,
> Take some time, you'll see,
> No fee, I'm free, just be with me.

The music thumping out of Ada went mostly quiet. Just the soft whisper of a bouncing rhythm. Ada stopped dancing, strode to the front of the stage and used simple gestures to finish.

> Humans, robots changing trends,
> It's not a game of us vs. thems,
> I see a future, there are no ends,
> I see hope, you're all my friends.

The gentle music rolled into an echo around the hall and then shut off. I could hear Li breathing slowly and saw 10 quickly scan the crowd.

Why was everyone quiet?

Then, an explosion of cheering and applause. The hall shook.

"Yoooooooooooooooooooooooooowindoooooo!" yelled Li, dancing around with 10.

Ada gave a curtsy, then a bow, then pointed at Li and did a full body rotating thumbs-up.

"Li, that was amazing. It totally worked, and everyone loved it," I said, giving Li a huge hug.

"Let's hope the judges feel the same way," 10 said, as the scores were handed to Principal Tajek and he walked over to the microphone.

"Ok, scores for Ada for part one, creative. Oh, well. Interesting," Principal Tajek said, as I closed my eyes yet again. "Twenty-five points."

The crowd went wild, and our team went a little wilder.

"Twenty-five. Twenty-five. Twenty-five!" I yelled as I twirled Li around and around.

"Technically, that's the first twenty-five in history. Amazing. Wonderful. Just… Just… Just… Yooooooowindooo!" 10 yelled.

I flung my arms around Ada's shoulders, grabbed Li and 10, and pulled them into a very tight hug.

"You did it," I said.

"We did it. That was fun," Ada said. "Thank you, Li."

"Oh, why thank you so much, it was a pleasure working with you," Li said, bowing into a spin.

"We haven't done it yet. But it's a very good start. And Dalk, well, he must be squirming in his tight, black pants," 10 said with an ear-to-ear smirk.

Oh my. One breath at a time. One step at a time. Two more big steps to go. But it was certainly game on.

T-Minus Three

School Robot Competition
Day Two, Part Two: Mental

9:45 a.m.
Fifteen minutes to start of competition

"Welcome everyone to day two of the robot competition." Mrs. D'Silva's voice rang out over the speakers. "Please get your metallic friends into position and we can get started."

Today the hall was set up with eight stations in a semicircle, one for each robot. At the open end stood a microphone next to a projector, spraying light onto a screen. All it said at the moment was "Day Two."

I was trying to ignore the leftover nausea. A few minutes ago I was vomiting in the playground. Luckily, Li and 10 calmed my frazzled nerves and we ran back inside just in time.

The robots took up their positions. Ukko and Ada were directly opposite each other. Behind Ukko, I could see Dalk busy working with his team. His hair seemed extra messy today and his eyes looked red and tired. Today he looked more stressed than confident.

Maybe I was getting to him after all.

The full leaderboard was shown on the screen.

Position	Team	Day 1 Creative: Score
1	Ada	25
2	Ukko	22
3	Sharks With Lasers	20
4	Deckard	19
5	Astro Dude	18
6	Tiger	17
7	HAL 45.3	16
8	Ozone	11

"For all of you new people jumping on the wonderful robotics bandwagon, welcome. Day two is all about the brains. We will ask the robots five riddles at the same time and they must each submit their answer within sixty seconds. The responses come wirelessly into the main computer and, once the time is up, we'll show them on the screen along with the correct answer. Each correct solution is worth five points and the riddles get harder and harder as we go along," Mrs. D'Silva announced. "There is also an app for this if you want to play along. Is everyone ready for the first riddle?"

The crowd chorused a "yeah" and some of the robots gave exuberant gestures of confidence.

"Riddle number one…"

> If you could see my face,
> You would know that I'm
> Handing you a gift
> You will love in time.

The riddle is displayed on a timer counting down from sixty seconds. Exclamations of glee ripple through the crowd as they work it out.

"All answers are locked in," Mrs. D'Silva said. "And the answer is…clock!" She then displayed all the robots' answers and they all got it right. Five points across the board.

"Riddle two…"

> Don't go looking, you can't see me,
> But I make it hard to climb or throw a ball.
> The bigger you get, the harder I work,
> I'm a force and I'll make you fall.

"Sixty, fifty-nine, fifty-eight…five, four, three, two, one! With all answers locked in, this one is of course…gravity! Oh, Sharks With Lasers didn't get the correct answer. Ba bowww. Well done to the rest of you clever processors."

"Two for two, a good start, team," 10 said.

I heard 10 but was too nervous to do anything but make too many *click click click* noises with my tongue.

Ada turned around and gave a circular motion thumbs-up.

"Let's step it up a notch," said Mrs. D'Silva. "Riddle three…"

> I helped build early computers,
> And I help clean your home,
> Some people say I'm nothing,
> In space I'm all alone.

Wow, that's much harder. I certainly don't know it.

I covered my eyes and made small groaning noises. After the minute counted down, Mrs. D'Silva unveiled the answer to the third riddle: a vacuum.

Sharks With Lasers got it wrong again, as well as Tiger and Ozone. Ada, Ukko, Deckard, and HAL 45.3 answered the first three correctly.

Li leaped onto my lap after a shriek of relief to the ceiling.

"This is like an eight-way penalty shoot-out," 10 said, with nervous laughter. "We're three for three." Ada's torso displayed a graphic of a soccer billowing the back of a net and fireworks spraying.

"Now it's really super-duper level time. Riddle four," Mrs. D'Silva said.

> I'm fast,
> Love mirrors,
> I bounce,
> All colors.

The hall filled with looks of strained confusion. I flicked between Ada, putting my head between my legs, looking at the roof, and then back at Ada. 10 seemed to enjoy the stress, crouching down and watching all the robots processing it. Li was taking photos, though the robots weren't really doing anything.

"Time's up," called Mrs. D'Silva. "Lock in your answers. This is where we separate the ENIACs from the 486s. Ok, all locked in. The answer...to riddle four...is...the following word..."

"Just say it!" I yelled out, much to everyone's surprise, then I hid my head under a towel.

"Whoa, maybe a little too much tension in the room. Without further ado, the answer is...light! And here are the robots' answers," Mrs. D'Silva said.

I heard muffled cheers, but I still had my head covered with my fingers in my ears.

"What happened? Don't tell me. Ok, tell me. No, don't tell me," I said.

Sitting on the chair, looking at the ground, I saw Li lying down, shimmying into my view with two thumbs-up. I stood up, shuffled over Li and gave a big fist pump to the sky.

"Eeeeeeee," I yelled, and then pulled back. I hated it when I squealed. I at least wanted three right, but what I secretly wanted was four. I hugged Li and 10 so tight, our heads hit and we gave a joint "Owww."

Ada leaned forward and looked out between spread legs at me, and I turned around and did the same. Lucia was beaming with pride. Dasan had taken about six hundred photos and videos from a phone and two cameras.

Ukko was the only other bot to get it right and Dalk was half-cheering, not happy we were keeping it so close.

The final question was always a combination of cryptic, complex, and obscure. It had never been answered correctly in the history of the competition.

"Here we are, folks," Mrs. D'Silva said. "The toughest of the toughest. Let's roll...for riddle five, to add to the tension, each robot will lock in their answer, and then reveal them one at a time."

"Riddle five."

There is no end to this traveler...

Everyone waited for her to continue.

"That's it. Sixty seconds starts now," said Mrs. D'Silva.

"Huh?" asked 10. "Is that really a riddle? It's more of a statement. I've never seen one like it. Well, at least no one is going to get it."

"That can't be right? How do you even start?" I asked. "Li, do you know what it is?"

"This is way out of my most purple thoughts, but I love it," Li said.

"Well, let's hope that Ada loves it, too," I said.

The crowd chanted "Five, four, three, two, one." You could almost hear the robots sigh with relief.

"Ok, locked in, we are going to go from bottom to top to see who got this right," said Mrs. D'Silva. "Up first, Ozone, answer, Marco Polo…incorrect. HAL 45.3, answer, orbit…incorrect, but nice try. Tiger, answer, walking…incorrect. Astro Dude, answer, 'I refuse to answer on the grounds that I may incriminate myself'…uhhh, ok, that's incorrect and I'm pretty sure you just did. Sharks With Lasers, answer, energy…incorrect. Ukko, answer, the equator…"

I saw Dalk close his eyes and ball his hands into fists.

"Incorrect," Mrs. D'Silva confirmed with gusto. Dalk kicked a chair. "And last but certainly not least, we have Ada, answer, wheel…"

10, Li, and I held hands and tried to breathe.

"Correct. It's correct. For the first time ever, we have a five-for-five, twenty-five-point robot. Amazing!" Mrs. D'Silva sang out, dancing from foot to foot.

The crowd went nuts. Lucia, Dasan, and the team in the grandstands jumped up and flung high-fives, hugs, and "yeahs" around with reckless abandon. On the hall floor, we picked up Ada in our arms and spun around cheering.

"Yes, it was brilliant. My circuits are overwhelmed," Ada said, back of hand to forehead.

"You don't get dizzy, Ada. I programmed that!" 10 said, laughing at Ada's cheekiness.

Our celebration was interrupted by a loud crash. I saw Dalk
disappearing through the slammed doors.

*He is really losing it. I guess he's never been behind like this before.
I mean, underneath all that black clothing, he's still a kid.*

"Ok, ok, here is the score update after day two. It is very, very
good," Principal Tajek said, trying very, very hard to be as energetic as
Mrs. D'Silva, but failing. Though with everyone staring at the screen
and the noise, he may have felt otherwise.

	Creative	Mental	Total
Ada	25	25	50
Ukko	22	20	42
Deckard	19	15	34
HAL 45.3	16	15	31
Sharks With Lasers	20	10	30
Tiger	17	10	27
Astro Dude	18	5	23
Ozone	11	10	21

"I can't believe it," said 10, standing still, talking to herself.
"Eight points up on Dalk after day two. Eight points up. Technically,
tomorrow, if we win the physical part, or even just come second, or
just beat Dalk, then we win. I can't believe it. I really can't believe it."

"I can't believe how much fun I'm having indoors. Being in a
team is awesome," Li said, walking backward in a circle.

I just kept hugging Ada. "I'm so proud of you. You did
amazingly. How did you work that out?" I asked.

"It was all of you who helped," Ada replied. "Your data sources,
AZ; your creative sources, Li; and your challenging philosophical
questions, 10. I have also reached my quota of hugs today, though I
know Li says I can't have too many, I have a big race tomorrow…"

The rest of the team joined them on the hall floor with a few
more hugs and congratulations.

"Regardless of what happens tomorrow, I'm proud of all of you. Without you, we wouldn't even have made it to day one. Thank you. I'm just not sure how this day can get any better," I said.

"Well, I might try," Katrin said. "I just got a call from the hospital and Matias has regained consciousness. He's doing fine and should make a full recovery."

"That's fantastic," I yelled, throwing my arms around her.

There was something new here. I could feel it. The sense of wild hope was replaced by a sense of actual belief.

"Technically, we're only two-thirds of the way through the competition. We should get started on preparation for tomorrow," 10 said.

"Yes, you're right. We want to finish strong. Let's get to work," I said, and the crew immediately fell into a buzzing flow of activity. 10, Jerel, and Dasan were going to stay in the lab with Ada to ensure nothing happened overnight.

I said 10 should go home for a good night's sleep, given the work she'd have to do tomorrow, but she insisted on staying with Ada. "I'm not sure I'll be able to sleep anyway," she said.

I left the crew and went home to look at the ceiling. I replayed the last two days over and over.

That felt amazing. Did it really happen? Did we really do all that? We are doing it. We could really win this. Forget about the worst thing that can happen. What is the best *thing that can happen?*

I eventually fell asleep, then woke at 7:20 a.m. to a text message:

Hi AZ, I've been a real jerk. I want to explain why. I can't meet publicly. Please meet at my uncle's house at the end of Station Road at eight o'clock. It's important. I don't want anyone to get hurt again. Dalk

T-Minus Two

I spent a few minutes rereading the text and thinking about what I should do.

He has been stressed. I bet it's his dad. If there is a chance to avoid another incident, then I should take it. If anyone got hurt again and I didn't do anything then I'd never forgive myself.

Today's competition didn't start until ten o'clock and Station Road wasn't too far out of my way. I hopped on my bike, rode across town and down Station Road to a big house. The gate looked pretty old and was a bit rusted. I pressed an intercom button and heard a staticky *beeeep*. After a few seconds of silence, it crackled to life.

"Hello, AZ? Is that you?" Dalk's voice came out of the speaker.

"Um, yes, what is this about? I need to get to the competition. And so do you," I said.

"Yeah, I know. But I need to show you something first. It will only take a few minutes but after everything…I owe it to you. Come to the house." The gate jerked open and the intercom went silent.

I stood for a long minute facing down the long driveway. As a precaution, I enabled tracking on the security app Adewale had given us all. I rode slowly down to a very large, quiet house. The looping driveway was empty of cars. I dropped my bike down and stepped up toward the front door and was about to knock when it opened. Dalk appeared in the doorway, his usual, confident demeanor was gone.

"Hey AZ, I'm glad you came. I'm really sorry for the cloak and dagger. You have no idea what my life is really like. Honestly, all the money isn't worth all the stress," Dalk said.

"What is this about? You haven't said anything but nasty things to me and now you want to chat. I need to be with my team," I said, not moving.

"I know. Sorry I've been so horrible. It's my dad. He has this thing and, well, it's easier if I show you. It will only take a minute and then we can get to the competition. But you need to promise not to tell anyone, ok?" Dalk said from the doorway.

"I'm not promising anything," I said.

"Ok, ok, sure, I understand," he said, rubbing his eyes and scratching the back of his head.

He's a mess.

I took a breath and followed Dalk. He opened a door off the hallway to a stairway. He flicked on a light and walked down the stairs. "Seriously, it will just take a minute and it will explain everything."

This was getting stranger by the minute. I checked my phone; it was 8:23 a.m. and the security app was still tracking me. I sent a beacon notice out. If I didn't deactivate it within ten minutes, it would alert the team and they would know my exact position. I walked down the stairs.

The room he indicated hadn't been cleaned for a while and seemed full of junk.

Dalk was standing in front of what looked like an old computer. It was a beige cube, about forty centimeters tall with two thin slots in the front and an old silver sticker, peeling at the corners.

"What do you want to show me, Dalk? This seems really weird."

"Just read what it says on that sticker. It will make it all clear," Dalk said.

I took a few steps forward, leaned down, and looked at the sticker.

" 'Computer repairs? Call 8—' " I started, when Dalk suddenly pushed me from behind. I lost my balance and rolled onto the ground, crashing into the computer and some shelves. I looked up to see Dalk running up the stairs.

It's a trap! I'm in trouble. He's going to lock me in here and Ada will be disqualified. How could I be so gullible?

I got up and ran after him. I was halfway up the stairs when the door slammed shut.

Don't panic. Stay calm.

I grabbed the door handle. Left, right. Left, right, left, right, left, right.

"I'm sorry, AZ," came Dalk's voice from the other side of the door.

I let my hand fall to my side, and a feeling of hopelessness swept over me.

I started pleading, "Let me out. Open this door now. Dalk, please don't do this, I need to get to the competition. Locking me in here is just crazy. You might win but it's only because you've cheated. You haven't actually beaten me."

"I'm sorry, AZ. I'm sorry," Dalk said through the door.

It sounded like he was crying. *I'm the one locked in here? Why is he crying?*

"It's not me. It's not. You don't know what is at stake. You don't know what it means. I don't… I don't… You just need to stay here a few hours and your team will be disqualified. It's not your fault, AZ. It's not Ada. It's not me. It's the plan," his head banged against the door as he spoke.

"Then don't do it, Dalk. Just open the door. Maybe I can help you," I said, trying to reason with him.

My thoughts were split. One part scared to death. One part calm.

"You can't. No one can. I'm sorry," his voice trailed off and I heard footsteps clip-clop to silence.

I was alone.

Is this really happening? Ada gets smashed, then I'm expelled, and now I'm stuck in the basement of an old house and we're going to be disqualified. And it's my own fault for going against my instincts.

No. Questions and rage come later. Action comes now. This was the new me and this is not how it ends.

I hit the door hard with my shoulder a few times. *It's strong. I'm not getting through there.*

I grabbed my phone. I had no service or data coverage. It was 8:47 a.m. My beacon should send an alert in seven minutes.

Oh jeez. Deep breaths. Focus your eyes. Focus your mind. What do you see? There are no other doors. There is one window. It's high.

About three meters up. Too high to jump to. It looks like it's welded shut. It's still my only hope. What's in this basement?

Inventory check:

- Brooms
- Plastic and metal buckets
- Tools
- Old house bricks
- Pipes sticking out of walls
- An old computer
- Paint brushes and tins
- Spray paint cans
- Candles

- Metal funnel
- Rags
- Duct tape
- Matches
- A few lengths of rope
- A fire-retardant blanket
- A fire extinguisher
- Piles of garbage

There was one thin pipe coming out from under the window. I climbed onto it and jumped up and grabbed the ledge. The pipe wouldn't hold my weight for long. The window was welded shut. I needed to open it first. I jumped down to the ground.

Brooms and candles? Not useful.

Rope and spray can? Not useful.

Matches? Not useful. ,

Think. Think. Think.

Rope…bricks…bricks on the rope, swing the rope, smash the window. Yes. That could work.

I tied a brick with rope. Swing, miss, swing, miss, swing, hit, swing miss, swing hit, swing hit, swing miss, swing smash. Shattered glass sprayed the room.

Keep moving.

I carefully stepped onto the pipe coming out of the wall and reached up to the ledge. I pushed off with my foot to jump up and reached out to freedom.

The pipe snapped off. I fell back to the ground hard. I sat up. The pipe was completely ripped out. *There goes my booster.*

But what's that sound? What's that smell?

Gas!

I could smell gas pouring out of the hole where the pipe snapped off. The room was getting filled with it. That could suffocate me or maybe even ignite.

I wedged a bit of rag into the hole as best I could, but it was still seeping out. I needed to get out of here fast.

Ok, how do I get up there? I wondered. I couldn't climb now. Nothing would stack high enough to climb on. The ropes couldn't hold onto anything.

How about propulsion? A fire extinguisher! But is it strong enough? I needed a vehicle, a sturdy one. The metal bucket. A metal funnel to focus the stream. I could sit on the blanket on top of the bucket, then set off the extinguisher, fling myself into the air, grab the window ledge, and climb out. Risks? A lot. It could be a bad angle, there would be broken glass, nothing to cushion my fall, and…ok, enough risk evaluation, there were no other options.

Extinguisher taped to the funnel and bucket. Pull pin out of extinguisher, blanket ready, rags wound around hands. Fail. Couldn't pull extinguisher trigger. Unwound rope into string, tied around trigger, back onto bucket, back on the bucket, ready. Breathe. Breathe. Breathe. Ready. Squeeze. "Whoaahh…"

The aim is off, and I shot off backward, into a wall of junk. My head, arm, and back started to throb painfully.

This room is filling with gas. Come on.

I got up and back on the bucket. *Breathe. Breathe. Ready. SQUEEZE.*

My aim was better, straight up, but not quite there. I was almost to the roof and twisted my body forward to avoid smashing my head against the wooden beams. My back hit it squarely and for an instant I was suspended in the air.

Then I fell. My stomach hit the bucket.

As I fought to not pass out, I realized the gas smell was almost overpowering me.

Clear the area. Put the equipment back together. Step on the bucket. Breathe. Ready. Squeeze.

I got up. I let go of the string, I went up, near the window, I reached out, I grabbed, I scratched, I held.

"Yes!" I actually squealed out loud. The squeal became a scream as the broken glass cut through my fingers and into my hand. My good hand. It released from the edge. Blood dripped to the floor. I was dangling. If I let go, it would be over. I couldn't hold on long.

"This is not over," I said out loud.

My foot found a bump in the wall. Small, but just enough to give me some leverage.

I pushed on it, thought of Ada, screamed, and threw myself up with all my will and all of my rage. My hand found an edge outside the window and I pulled. Glass cut me as I dragged myself through the tiny space. *Pull. Lift yourself. Pull. Pull.* My eyes closed but through my eyelids I saw a dark red light and the smell of roses flooded my lungs as I gasped for air.

That gas could still ignite. I need to get clear of this house.

One more pull and I was out. Dirt mixed with blood. Adrenaline mixed with blood.

I'm out.

I got up.

Get clear. Get safe.

I saw a pond twenty meters away. Risks? Sharp fountain spouts, it could be too shallow. No other options. I ran.

Behind me the house exploded. Panic and stillness. Terror filled my ears and my mind. I jumped and I was in a white-hot wind. My skin and hair were hot. I hit the water and sunk to the bottom. Above me, red and white fire filled the air. The fire was heating the water. I wasn't fast enough.

I thought of Ada's hands. Strong and precise. Filled with tiny circuits and endless ones and zeros. That first time Ada reached out with a hand for mine. We didn't program Ada to do it. Ada wanted to. Ada wanted to hold my hand.

T-Minus One

School Robot Competition
Part Three: Physical

Power: On
Battery level: 100%
BIOS loaded
Initialization tests complete
Condition report: 100%
Ada: Advanced cybernetic robot, powered up
8:37:51 a.m.

10 initiates me today. The previous two days it was AZ. 10 continues to use her laptop to run my unit tests.

"Good morning, Ada. A big day today," 10 says to me.

"Good morning, 10. Yes, the final day of the competition," I say.

Li walks in and gives me a big morning hug.

Thirteen minutes and twenty-eight seconds pass.

"Where is AZ?" Li asks.

"It's not like her to be late. I'll text her," 10 says.

Six minutes and nine seconds pass. One hour, nine minutes, and forty-two seconds until the competition starts.

The rest of the team is here now and helping with final preparations. Someone checks the door every 17.85 seconds on average. The team is worried.

"Ada, do you know where AZ is?" Li asks me.

"I have had no communication from her; her beacon has not been activated," I say.

At 9:04:51 a decision is made to take more actions to find AZ. 10 tries calling her again but there was no answer. Lucia drove Jerel and Maureen to her house. Adewale had checked the security beacons again but nothing has been received.

No one can find her.

It was 9:58. Two minutes to go. The door burst open. Jerel, Maureen, and Lucia walk in. They join the rest of the team in the stands. "Any sign of her?" Lucia calls out, face showing fear.

"No, no sign," Li says quietly.

I am more worried about AZ than the competition. She is important to me forever. The competition is important to me only because it is important to her and the team.

It is 9:59 a.m. One minute to go. Li has started crying.

"This can't be how it goes. It can't be," 10 says.

I can calculate the sadness.

The door swings open with a crash.

There is AZ. She is dirty, cut, bleeding and, based on her elevated heart rate and rapid breathing, she is very tired. She holds onto the doorframe. She made it.

I stepped into the hall with the little energy I had left. Before anyone could react, I scanned the room and locked eyes with Dalk. The message my eyes sent was crystal clear.

I am as determined as white-hot fire and I will not be denied.

His face looked like it would shatter, until he turned away.

The hall erupted into activity and noise.

Ada and 10 sprinted toward me. Li screamed. My parents ran down the stairs with the rest of Ada's team. Dalk hid his head in his hands.

Ada reached me first and caught me as I fell in strong arms. "Are you ok? What happened to you?"

"I had an...accident, but I'm ok," I said. "Just get me to our station."

"You need to go to a hospital. You may have serious injuries," 10 said, helping support my other side.

A circle formed around me, with everyone talking at the same time.

"AZ, we need to call an ambulance. You're hurt," my dad said.

"I'll be ok. We need to start the competition," I said, hobbling to our station with Ada and 10's help.

"AZ, listen to your father, you need to—" my mother said.

"Everyone, I know you're trying to look out for me. But this team worked so hard and has come so far, I can wait a few hours for some care, and then I'll go to the hospital. Honestly, I'm not really badly hurt. But I really badly want to finish this competition. Please just help me get through this." I pleaded and with a few more sighs of concern, everyone agreed.

"Let's go everyone, time to get…to work…" I said over the top of my mother, walking past her and gasping at every second step.

"I've got a first aid kit here, we can patch you up a bit," 10 said, sensing, and I'm guessing partly hoping, my determination would see us through. "What happened to you? Who did this?"

Jax burst into the circle, "*Disqualified*. She's too late. It was 10:01 by my watch and I'm never late," Jax yelled at Principal Tajek.

"Ok, ok, let's sort this out. Maybe she was late, maybe, yes, maybe," Principal Tajek started.

"Ahh, no. Let's not maybe or 'ok,' " Mrs. D'Silva interjected. "The official clock was still showing 9:59 when the door opened. Do you agree, Mr. Jabari?"

"Yes, definitely. I was watching it when I heard the sound," Mr. Jabari said.

"She wasn't with her team. Disqualified!" said Jax.

Li was cleaning dirt off me and 10 was putting bandages on my cuts.

"She just has to be present in the hall. She's not disqualified. Now, let's get this competition going, if you please," Mrs. D'Silva said, eyeball-to-eyeball with Jax.

Principal Tajek shrugged and squinted in apology. Jax grumbled his way over to Dalk, where they had a short, animated argument.

"AZ, you don't have to do this," Ada said, hand on my shoulder.

"I'll be fine and, yes, I do have to do this. I can tell you all about it after you win this race," I said, grabbing Ada's hand, feeling warmth from the hard, sleek surface.

What happened and what Dalk did was horrendous. But if I stop to deal with it right now, this moment will pass forever.

My parents and the team slowly made their way back up into the stands and the hall returned to its usual buzz.

"Wow, what a morning. And the race hasn't started yet," Mrs. D'Silva rallied over the speakers. "Robots, to the starting line."

The hall had undergone a dramatic transformation since yesterday. It'd been converted into an S-shaped course with a starting line at one end and a finish line at the other. In the middle were the four obstacles, which the robots had to navigate, and then a long sprint to finish.

"Well, I hope you're ready. This is definitely the hardest course I've ever seen. We'll be lucky to finish," 10 said.

"Technically, I'm the only one that has to finish," Ada said.

"Who programmed you to be so cheeky?" 10 asked.

"That would be me," Li said, hand raised proudly.

I almost smiled and checked out the course again. It was more than just hard. The physical section allowed some interaction with the team. They could send messages by voice or keyboard to guide their robot through the obstacles. Ada would still need the physical strength, flexibility, durability, and dexterity to make it through, but it would be a team effort.

"You've got this, Ada. You do. Don't forget to use race communication style," I said confidently.

"Affirmative," Ada said in a clear, loud voice.

Ada lifted a foot and gave a triple thumbs-up, spun, and strode over to the starting line along with the other robots. Ukko joined last, shoving others out of the way to make room. A quiet came over the hall.

This wasn't the preparation that I planned, but I'm learning that life is often about making the most of your circumstances.

"Ready…set…go!" called out Mrs. D'Silva.

The horror of the morning was gone. Replaced by the energy and excitement of this race starting. I watched in awe.

A cacophony of gears, actuators, and command-yelling teams crashed over the crowd, revving them to life. The robots ran, rolled, and tracked their way to the first obstacle, which was the leaning ladder. It was made of metal, about ten meters long, half a meter off the ground at the start and finished five meters higher. At the end was a bell, which had to be rung before a robot could move on.

The big challenge was that the ladders were not affixed on either end, so they could spin. Plus, there were only four ladders for eight robots.

Tiger reached the ladders quickest and used speed, getting about three-quarters of the way along before its momentum swung the ladder over. Instead of letting go, Tiger grabbed hold of the ladder and held on upside down and kept climbing.

Ukko arrived next, taking swift but measured movements up the second ladder. Ada and Astro Dude arrived and slowly started up the last two ladders.

Ozone got to the first ladder, with Tiger still climbing on the underside. Ozone almost immediately spun around and fell to the ground.

Deckard started up Ukko's ladder, then Ukko gave a big twist and spun the ladder completely around, throwing Deckard to the ground with a loud metallic crunch. There were no safety mats and Deckard hit hard, a shoulder taking most of the force and a leg twisting at angles. Deckard's team was furiously sending messages and communicating, willing their friend to get up. Deckard made a few crawls forward on one arm and then slumped to the ground. "Wake up, time to die," said the robot.

Ukko shuffled forward, reached out, and rang the bell. Dalk's team cheered loudly, but it was only Jax and his crew in the stands who joined them.

HAL 45.3 was scurrying up Ada's ladder. With Ada less than half a meter from the top, HAL 45.3 overbalanced and the ladder spun. Ada grabbed onto the ladder, but Ozone on the floor grabbed onto HAL 45.3, pulling the robot, who eventually let go. The motion sprung the ladder violently and Ada was knocked off. Ada's torso spun and Ada landed with a crash.

"Are you ok, Ada?" I asked through my comms earpiece.

"Yes, I am 96 percent operative, with 95 percent battery life. I need to start again," Ada replied.

HAL 45.3 got up and ran back to the same ladder and rang the bell.

"Ada, go up ladder two, it's empty," 10 suggested.

"Affirmative," Ada replied and started up the ladder again, this time a little faster, which was risky. But Ukko was already approaching the second obstacle.

On ladder one Ozone overbalanced, and Tiger was able to move forward and ring the bell. At the bottom of the fourth ladder, after knocking each other off twice, Astro Dude and Sharks With Lasers were both fighting to climb up first.

Ada then made it to the top and rang the bell. Dropping to the ground and continuing along the track, Ada could see the second obstacle: the water. Anticipating my concerns, Ada said, "I don't believe any damage I have sustained will affect my submersion."

"Good," I said, trying to sound confident. 10 didn't seem so sure.

Obstacle two was a round, plastic pool about two meters in diameter and two meters deep. The walls were an almost-clear plastic blue and at the bottom were eight house bricks. The robots had to dive in, retrieve a brick from the bottom, and get out.

Ukko arrived first and took a running leap over the side, landing with a neat dive into the water. Tiger followed right behind, running up and over the wall. HAL 45.3 used suction cup-like devices on its arms and legs to scale the wall.

"Good job on the ladder, Ada, you're doing great," I said over the comms channel. "Get your pace up to twenty-five kilometers per hour and you can easily make that lip."

"Roger, over."

Five meters out from the pool, Ada's arms lifted into the air and quickly circled back to the ground. Ada started tumbling fast, then, a meter out, sprang up, somersaulted, and dove into the pool. Ada's team in the stands applauded loudly.

Next to me I sensed 10 wince. Even the smallest leak could lead to a short-circuit, ending Ada's race. 10's computer flashed red as an alarm beeped.

"Is it bad?" Li asked.

"Hmmm, noooo. No, it doesn't look too bad. Technically, it's a malfunctioning actuator. Ada's left shoulder won't have full 360-degree freedom of movement. It should be ok," 10 said.

"I am 94 percent operative, with 87 percent battery life," Ada said.

I kept focused, and watched Ukko grab a brick from the bottom of the pool. Ukko turned around and kicked up directly toward Ada.

"Evade," I yelled.

Ukko aimed the brick for Ada's head, but Ada spun away, and it missed by nanometers. Our team slumped back in relief.

Ukko breached the water as HAL 45.3 poked above the side of the pool wall. Ukko's brick connected with HAL 45.3's head and knocked it clean off. It sailed into the air and fell with a flat *thunk* three meters away.

The crowd jeered.

"Is that allowed?" Li asked.

"You are not allowed to deliberately damage another robot, but if in the course of the race there is physical contact, then it's survival of the strongest," 10 replied.

Ukko climbed out of the pool and past the headless robot, then dropped the house brick next to HAL 45.3's head and ran off to the next obstacle.

HAL 45.3's body let go of the pool edge, dropped to the ground, walked over and picked up its own head. "This is highly irregular," HAL 45.3 said and ended the race.

Ada picked up a brick, then noticed Tiger struggling to grasp another one.

"I want to help Tiger," Ada said over the comms.

"Do it," I said. Li nodded approval and 10 shrugged her shoulders.

Ada picked up a brick and handed it to Tiger, who was able to hold it with both arms. Together they pushed for the surface. Tiger jumped out quickly and waited for Ada on the ground, and together they ran to the next challenge.

Obstacle three, set halfway down the middle of the S-shaped course, was about jumping. The robots had to get to the top of a red, hard plastic sphere about a meter across and then leap through a one-meter-wide, five-meter-high metal hoop, that was also set on fire. It was a test of strength, agility, and confidence.

Ukko was on top of the sphere, slowly rising from bent knees, as Ada and Tiger approached.

"Ada, do you know why Ukko hasn't jumped yet?" I asked over the comms.

"I'm not sure. It appears that the ball is very smooth and slippery. There are no obvious handholds. This may be harder than we thought," Ada said.

Three meters out, Tiger ran on all fours and jumped for the ball. Ukko, seeing Tiger's impending arrival, turned quickly and jumped. Too quickly. One of Ukko's feet lost traction on the ball and this changed the trajectory of the jump. Ukko tried to adjust in mid-air but it wasn't enough. The crowd gasped as Ukko's left shoulder crashed into the flaming ring, sending the robot falling headfirst toward the floor. At the last second, Ukko curled into a ball and rolled over, bringing two strong feet down to land safely on the ground.

Ukko slowly extended up to full height from a crouch position. At the same time, Tiger landed on top of the ball and, using the momentum, sprung up toward the ring of fire. Ukko looked up to see Tiger sail through the ring, and land safely on the other side.

"Ada, can you jump like Tiger?" 10 asked.

"No. Two legs don't give the same balance points and my center of gravity will be too high," Ada said, climbing onto the ball and standing up.

> Definition: **Center of Gravity**—The point at which the entire weight of a body may be considered as concentrated so that if supported at this point the body would remain in equilibrium in any position.

"Be careful, Ukko is coming back," I warned.

"Got it."

I stood up to watch as a mess of robots converged on the sphere.

Ada bent and sprung into the air. Ukko jumped from the ground, reaching out for Ada. Seeing Ukko, Ada's legs angled back and up. Ukko missed Ada by millimeters, but the change of angle changed the flight path. Ada's head and body were through the ring when there was a clash of metal on metal. Ada's right leg slammed into the ring.

At the same time, Astro Dude was climbing to the top of the ball when Ukko landed directly on it. The crash directly on Astro Dude's head was a grinding mess. Astro Dude tilted back and crumpled against the ball. Sparks and parts flew. Ukko kicked Astro Dude's crushed body away.

"Game over, dude," Astro Dude said as the limp body slid down the ball and crashed to the floor.

The shock of the crowd was broken by the crash of Ada hitting the ground. Ada landed sideways, spinning torso taking the force and the body flipping over into a rough rollover. Ada ended up sliding to a stop, fully outstretched, looking up at the ceiling.

"Noooooo! Ada, are you ok? 10, is Ada ok?" I yelled.

"I'm checking, definitely some damage," 10 said.

Seconds ticked by and Ada lay still.

"I'm ok, it wasn't that bad, the roll protected me," said Ada. "I am 85 percent operative, with 68 percent battery life."

Ada had only just stood up when Ukko landed and charged. Ada jumped to the side and just managed to avoid being taken out. Ukko powered on as Ada flipped over and landed safely a few feet away.

Ada turned back and ran toward obstacle four, dexterity. The contraption looked complex with parts spinning, pushing, and lifting.

Running up the entryway, Ada looked at the first section. There were five fans about ten centimeters apart with blades spinning slowly, but in alternate directions and at different speeds.

Ukko went through the fourth blade with a clunk as it caught the black machine's arm.

"Ukko has taken a substantial hit. If my calculations are incorrect, I could fail," Ada said as Ukko went through the last blade unscathed.

"Technically, just calculate the spin speed and your required speed," 10 said, but Li's face looked doubtful.

"Close your eyes and feel your way through," Li said, and now 10's face looked doubtful.

"Do the math, trust your instincts, you can do it," I said.

Ada watched the blades' hypnotic blur and waited. And waited. And waited. Ukko was already halfway through the next dodging challenge.

Ada jumped, spun, twisted, and landed safely on the other side without a scratch.

"Eeeeeee. Yes, I'm squealing. Deal with it," I yelled, and winced as some of my own body's pain flooded through me.

Ukko looked around quickly and moved faster. The next part of the grinder looked even harder. A ten-meter corridor of moving columns, rolling bars, and spinning discs.

"No math here, these look random. You'll just have to react," I said.

Tiger was near the end of this part of the challenge, but it was clear that the obstacle had taken its toll. The lean, low-rising robot was moving slowly, almost dragging its back-left leg. Tiger tried to get out but was hit by a disc then knocked back by a column. Heavily shaken, the quadruped willed itself back up to standing. If Tiger could get through, there were fifty meters to the finish line and 25 points waiting. Assuming Ukko kept going to second for 20 points and Ada got third with 15 points, Ada would win the competition.

"Take your time, just don't get hurt," I said.

"The bars and discs may hurt, but you have to watch those columns," 10 said. "They will end your race."

"Copy that," said Ada, moving into the maze, dodging a rectangular block that came out from the wall and all the way across to connect with the other side.

Ukko made it past a tough section that Ada was about to face. There was a large spinning disc taking up the whole corridor in front of two wide columns. There wasn't much room between them and the double columns almost crushed Ukko's leg.

Ada was about to shoot past the big, spinning disk when Tiger lunged forward, bounced off a moving bar and clumsily rolled out of the obstacle and into the clear.

Ukko looked back at Ada. I looked over at Dalk and saw him yell into his comms piece.

"It's a trap!" I yelled, one moment too late.

Ada leaped past the spinning disc and into the target zone of the two colliding columns. Ukko stepped back and blocked the path to safety.

The spinning disc came up and now Ada was caught. No way back and, when the columns come out, Ada will be hit. Thanks to super-fast reflexes, Ada instantly pushed against Ukko's body with all available strength. The contraption whirred, as the two columns emerged from the wall. A vision of Ada completely crushed flashed through my mind and tore at my heart.

Out of nowhere, Tiger slammed into the back of Ukko's knees. With Ada pushing Ukko's chest, the big robot fell backward. Ada scrambled into the free space but was dealt a heavy blow to the left knee. Ada hit the ground and rolled to a sideways kneeling position.

Tiger lay at Ukko's feet as the two columns receded into the wall. Ukko pulled back both legs and pushed the beaten-up robot into the target zone. Then, seeing what Ukko was doing, Ada sprung out an arm to grab Tiger's leg. It was too late. The two columns smashed together with Tiger in the middle, filling the room with the grind of broken metal and a smell of burning electrics. The columns then moved back, leaving Tiger to slowly slip to the ground, a few LEDs blinking, barely moving.

I looked to Tiger's team, faces shocked with sadness.

"You know what you should do," I said to Ada.

"Thank you." Ada picked up the near-lifeless shell of Tiger and said, "Thank you for saving me, Tiger."

"What's your condition?" 10 asked into the comms mic.

"I am 44 percent operational, with 23 percent battery life," Ada replied.

By this time, Ukko had dived out of the last challenge and rolled clear. Ukko then stood up, looked back at Ada carrying Tiger, then turned to the finish line. I knew that Ada couldn't catch up now. Ukko raised both arms in triumph and started to jog, looking to the crowd for acknowledgment, which only came from Dalk's team and Jax.

Suddenly, a two-meter bar sprung up and swung toward Ukko. The competition designers had created a final test of dexterity. The bar caught Ukko on the left shoulder, forcing the robot onto the ground. Ukko was pinned and Dalk's team panicked.

The whole room seemed alive with tension, anticipation, and energy.

Ukko struggled on the ground. Ozone and Sharks With Lasers had finally made it to the fourth obstacle and perhaps saw their chance for a high-place finish. They both started through the metal meat grinder.

Ada, still carrying Tiger, jumped and rolled through the final section of the grinder. Cradling Tiger, Ada stood up and checked the ground for more surprises. Edging forward, Ada saw and heard Ukko struggling to push the bar off. Seeing Ada approaching, Ukko tried another big effort but failed.

"Get this off me. Now," Ukko said. "Please."

"It's up to you, Ada," I said through the comms piece.

The whole hall was quiet, but for the whirl of the contraptions and the occasional clunk of Ozone and Sharks With Lasers. Ada walked up to Ukko, stopped, and looked down at the struggling machine. "You don't deserve it. But I will help you," Ada said.

"Thank you, thank you, Ada," Ukko said.

"After I take Tiger across the line. Tiger definitely deserves it," Ada said, looking up and walking on.

"No. Now. Help me now," Ukko yelled.

The tension wrenched me in all directions. 10 and Li stood next to me, clearly struggling with the enormity of the situation. Slowly sinking in was the fact that Ada was about to win.

"If Ada carries Tiger across the line it might technically be a tie. It doesn't matter, though. First or second, we will win," 10 said.

I wanted to talk. Wanted just to know what to say. Nothing came out. I couldn't feel the pain in my leg and hands, but I could feel the hearts and engines of every person and robot in the hall. It filled me and it emptied me. I needed to cry but not yet.

"Let's finish this, Ada," I said.

Ada kept stepping forward. Slowly. Damaged. Hurt. The finish line just five meters away.

I looked at Dalk. His eyes burned like fury, his lips in a twisted grin, he held a tablet in one hand and jabbed down on it with his finger.

"Oh no," I said, my body instantly responding and launching into a run. I didn't know what was about to happen, but I knew it wouldn't be good.

Ada took another step toward the finish. Three meters away. A new voice filled the room. It was robotic, dark, and echoed off the walls like madness.

"Enemy located. Multiple units," said the voice. It came from Ukko, but it sounded completely different. "Engage."

From each of Ukko's shoulders emerged two devices. On the left, a silver cube with a red dot on one side. On the right, a black cylinder. Both devices pivoted and pointed at the bar holding the robot down. The air crackled with energy as a blast emerged from the left device. The bar buckled and Ukko stood and faced Ada. The two devices spun and aimed directly at Ada and Tiger.

My eyes saw but couldn't comprehend. I ran as fast as I could, even though I knew I wouldn't make it in time. The air crackled again, and I felt like I'd just blown out my last match on a pitch-black night.

T-Minus Zero

At the sound of the first crackling and hiss, Ada had turned around and saw the bar melted and buckled.

Ada's systems and my brain tried to process the situation at the speed of light. The noises. The actions. The scenarios. What had happened. What could happen.

I was running, fear driving me, but no hope in my heart. It was happening too fast. I saw people running from the gym, I heard their screams.

I was twenty-five meters away.

The weapons on Ukko's shoulders spun back toward the grinder. The one on the left crackled and spat a red beam of laser. Ozone dove left and rolled behind the grinder's wall. The laser beam hit Sharks With Lasers full on the chest and the robot was flung backward into the grinder. A spinning disc and column severed the robot in two and crushed its head. Sparks flew high into the air.

The weapon on Ukko's right shoulder glowed blue, made a sound like a huge bass drum, and shot a white circle of light. An instant later, it thumped into Ozone's leg, which immediately went still. The paralysis spread up through the robot and it slumped down, face-first, quiet.

I was twenty meters away.

In the few seconds it took Ukko to take out the robots, I saw Ada do three things. Ada put Tiger on the floor. Ada sent a distress signal via all communication channels. Ada dove behind the pool.

Ukko strode forward toward the finish line, aimed at the pool, and fired a red laser beam. The pool wall shattered, spraying glass in all directions. The water held the pool's form for a nanosecond, collapsed and gushed out in waves across the floor.

I was ten meters away.

Ada was moving before the first drop of water hit the ground, running for the big ball from obstacle three. Ukko marched toward the finish line, weapons spinning toward Ada, and fired a white ball of light. Ada ran, knowing if the white light connected it would all be over. The ball of light caught the very edge of the silver ball and bounced harmlessly away.

"You must stop Ada," Dalk yelled into his comms piece.

Unbelievable. He's still thinking about winning the competition. Coming second will still mean Ada won on points.

Ukko stopped, turned, and walked toward Ada. Ada charged straight into the first section of the grinder. Ukko got to the end of the grinder, which was still partly blocked by the pieces of Sharks With Lasers.

Ada took cover behind a column, but it slid back away, forcing a quick move to a wide bar coming down from the roof. Ukko shot a laser beam and it hit the bar, sending a spray of sparks dancing off in all directions. The bar sagged and the whole grinder stopped. No other columns or discs appeared. Ada was completely open.

The air crackled with energy again as Ukko prepared to shoot. At the last second, I made it to Ukko and put my hand over the laser. It fired and I screamed. I fell forward onto Ukko, and we lost balance and fell toward the mouth of the grinder. I pushed with my legs and scrambled free.

Ukko sat up and I saw the laser point directly at me, less than a meter away. The air crackled with energy.

Ada landed on Ukko with desperate force. The two robots intertwined as the laser beam shot, bounced, smoldered. A shrill sound of metal shearing and echoing off the walls of the now mostly empty gym.

10 and Li had arrived, pulling me back away from the battle.

"No, leave me, I have to help," I pleaded.

"AZ, your hand, your hand," Li said.

I looked down and saw my hand was a mangled mess.

"AZ, we have to get you out of here," 10 said, dragging me further away as I tried to scramble forward. The audience had already frantically begun to run for the exits.

I watched as Ada and Ukko wrestled at the end of the grinder, just two meters away. Ukko's legs kicked up and down to try and get Ada off. Instead, they connected with Sharks With Lasers's body, knocking it free of the column and disc it had wedged still. Released, the disc shot to life, spinning and cutting a swath of metal and sparks across the two robots, burning the air and slowing the melee. The column then came out from the wall, collecting Ukko's head and slamming it into the opposite wall, missing Ada by inches.

Someone had finally turned off the grinder and the hall grew horribly quiet, sirens wailing in the distance. Ada's full team had been blocked by the crowd from getting to the hall floor, but now made it through and ran toward them.

Most of Dalk's team had run out the door, but Dalk stood watching with a pained expression of disbelief on his face. Jax stood in the grandstands, shuffled down the stairs, and started walking to the door when Mrs. D'Silva blocked his way.

"Ada. Ada. Ada!" I yelled, as 10 and Li tried to get me to safety. "It's over, let me go, let me go."

10 and Li, seeing Ukko unmoving, let go of me and we all rushed to Ada. Our robot friend was lying at the edge of the grinder, among the crushed, fried electrics of both Ukko and Sharks With Lasers. When they were almost there, the lights on Ada's head lit up again.

"Don't touch me. Not yet. Please," Ada said, as we approached. "I want to finish this. I can do it. I am 18 percent operative, with 9 percent battery life. Please."

If anyone in the team touched the robot, they would be disqualified. My face contorted in confusion and pain as I looked at Ada and stepped back. 10 and Li stepped with me.

"I love you, Ada," I said, through tears.

"I love you, too," Ada replied.

Ada, legs severed by the disc, used both arms to pull clear of the tangled mess. Moving very slowly, Ada pulled toward the finish. The rest of the team arrived and formed a line on either side of the path.

"Technically, this is crazy, but you can do it," 10 said, clapping.

"You're in space, no friction, no gravity. Just flow," Li said, arms swinging around as if the extra brush of air pushed Ada.

"I am 16 percent operative, with 3 percent battery life," Ada said, less than a meter from the end.

Completely focused on Ada, I hadn't noticed that right next to the finish line lay Tiger's badly damaged body. Still active but barely.

"Ada, I want you to win this. You'll get a perfect score. Please," Tiger said, voice distorted by the frayed electronics.

"No, Tiger, you were going to win. You came back and saved me. You deserve it. I don't want a perfect score," Ada said.

Tiger, with a push from Ada and using every last ounce of energy and will, inched over the line and dropped to the floor.

Ada, still dragging with crushed arms, gave a last big pull and crossed the line. "I am 14 percent operative, with 0 percent battery life. Thank you team, we did it," Ada said, one arm buckling and crashing to the floor.

I rushed to Ada and hugged our broken robot.

"AZ, you need to get to the hospital now. You're really hurt," 10 said, hand on my shoulder. "We'll look after Ada."

I didn't move. I couldn't move.

Li leaned down. "AZ, Ada needs you to look after yourself now."

I nodded and pulled back from Ada's still body.

The room was suddenly full of police and paramedics. I saw Mrs. D'Silva half-blocking, half-wrestling Jax. When he saw the police, Jax stood still and surrendered.

Two paramedics arrived with a stretcher for me. They lifted me up and started pushing me quickly to the door.

"Ada!" I yelled. "Ada!"

I watched the scene slide away as I was rolled backward. The chaos. My team. Our robot.

T-Plus One

Three months later

B ack in our lab, I held the screwdriver in my hand, tried to turn it clockwise, and dropped it. That was my fourth time.

"This is going to take a while to get used to," 10 said, hovering annoyingly over my shoulder. "Technically, you have to learn the basics again."

Sighing with frustration, I held my new mechanical hand up to my eyes for about the thousandth time since it was attached a month ago. Ukko's laser had destroyed much of my muscles, tendons, and ligaments but left enough of my nerves. Lucia had called on a friend who was a world leader in robotic prosthesis and she was excited to work on me.

Definition: **Prosthesis**—An artificial device to replace or augment a missing or impaired part of the body.

I bent and straightened my new fingers. In many ways they were better than my old ones, but right now I felt like a one-year-old; clumsy and awkward.

I picked up the screwdriver and tightened the screw.

"I like it," Li said, sitting on a table nearby. "Now you can really have empathy for robots. You basically are one. A bit."

I walked, with my permanent limp, over to Li and we shared a big hug. "Thanks. I didn't really have a choice, but yeah, I kinda like it, too."

"Is everyone ready?" I yelled.

The whole team was here, including Lucia, Dasan, Mrs. D'Silva, Mr. Jabari, and Matias, who was out of the hospital and fitting in wonderfully.

There was a tone-clashed chorus of "Yes!"

After three weeks in the hospital, I had gone home and then straight to the lab to be with my friends. The crazy events on the last day of the competition had shocked everyone. We had started working through it together, knowing it would take time. Our bond had grown to a whole new level.

Dalk and Jax were arrested, but were released the same day thanks to a dozen lawyers. They blamed the house explosion on a gas leak and Ukko's actions on hackers. Dalk had my phone hacked so the security beacon had never been sent, and Jax had initiated a military mode in Ukko. Jax's media team spread hundreds of alternative stories about the day and a few weeks later the incident was largely forgotten.

I would not forget it.

Some deep, covert research uncovered that Jax Enterprises had been building robotic weapons for a number of armies around the world. I wrestled with the conflict that one robot could be made to kill, and another, like Ada, made to love.

What would Jax do next?

Despite Dalk's protests and Jax's threats to sue, Ukko was disqualified from the competition for violent behavior, not that it mattered. Tiger won the last challenge, Ada came second, and won the competition overall. Our team was happy when we were given the trophy but, with Ada in pieces, it didn't feel complete. Now it would.

"Go for it, 10," I said, kneeling down gently, watching, my robotic hand on my human heart.

I looked at the new Ada. Toes, legs, body, hands, arms, and head. Fear and excitement churned through me. They'd used as much of the old Ada as they could, plus a few new ideas. It felt like I was about to meet an old friend for the first time.

"Ok, here we go," 10 said, hitting a few keys on her keyboard.

Silence. Nothing happened.

A single LED blinked on Ada's head and our robot friend hummed to life.

"AZ," Ada said.

"Ada," I said, my vision blurring. "Welcome back. How do you feel?"

"I am 100 percent operative, with 100 percent battery life. How are you? You have a new hand. You are like me," Ada said.

"Yes, more than you know," I replied.

I wiped my eyes and felt my muscles get tense. I knew I was older now. Even more than just the days I had counted. All of me. My body, my mind, and my heart.

I thought back to how scared I was before all of this started. Scared just to try—in case I failed. Now, part of me is petrified about what I am capable of, and what I need to do next.

When I finished explaining my plan, I looked around the room to see faces of excitement and determination.

"Now let's get to work."

The Motherboard Puzzle Components

Acknowledgements

Thanks so much for reading this book. I hope you enjoyed it. If it inspired you even a little to dive into science, technology, engineering, and mathematics, then you've made me very happy.

If you have any questions, ideas for the sequel, stories to share, or if you solved the motherboard puzzle on page 50 (yes, it is solvable), please contact me at sbar@liubinskas.com. If you are looking for more inspiration, I have interviewed more than fifty women who work in STEM from around the world. Real-life inspirations: www.medium.com/shes-building-a-robot.

A big thanks to my kids for being my supporters and inspiration. Sam was the first to read it and Lucy and Grace were pivotal in my promotion. Also a huge thanks to my wife Karen for supporting me all the way through this crazy adventure. She backed me writing it in the first place, helped on the promotion campaign, and read it multiple times with wonderful feedback.

So why did I do all this? Well, one of my favorite things to do is read with my kids—I have two daughters and a son. I quickly felt that most of the main characters were male, especially the tough, strong, adventurous, brave and curious ones. I wasn't happy.

Then one day at a robotics panel at the SxSW (South by Southwest) conference, I ended up speaking to five women roboticists. I told them about my daughters and asked them how I could give them a good opportunity to get excited about technology when so many books seemed aimed at boys. They told me that the teenage years were really hard for them, as they had to fight against social pressure from friends, family and school systems to keep pursuing science, technology, engineering and mathematics (known as STEM).

I was struck by these inspiring role models and thought there should be more. I've always loved writing but had never written much more than blog posts, marketing material, and a workbook with my colleagues called Startup Focus. I wrote down some notes, which became an idea.

What if there was a strong female character who was into technology? Kind of like Hermione but, instead of magic, she uses tech, and instead of being in a supporting role, she's the champion. I was thinking a Hermione, combined with MacGuyver, combined with Grace Hopper. At the time, my kids and I were loving Robot Wars. So I took the inspiration from the roboticists and decided to build the story around a robot building competition.

The idea became an outline, then a plan, and then some chapters. I was plodding along until NaNoWriMo (National Novel Writing Month) coincided with a break in my work projects and I went for it. I went from half a book to a full book in one month. All done. Or so I thought.

When they tell you that finishing the book is halfway there and that the process takes years, you nod and say, "Sure, but I'll get it out faster." You'll be wrong. I shared the book with teenage girls, got some feedback, did a rewrite, ended up getting help from Mary Kole (who's literally wrote the book on writing for kids), she said I write a better voice in the first person, which lead to a big rewrite.

Then someone told me about Publishizer, which is a crowdfunding platform for books. Thank you to Kate Miller and the team at Publishizer who really get stuck in and help make the whole thing work. I decided to go for it while it was a lot of work in preparation and promotion, I sold 589 copies. My big supporters were Charlotte Yarkoni at Microsoft, Rob Casteneda from ServiceRocket, and the Sandstad family—thank you!

Here are all my other supporters—thank you all for making a huge commitment to me, the book, and the cause. Anne-Marie Elias, Carrie and Jesse Sandstad, Annie Parker, Nola and Bob Liubinskas, Brittany Maalona, Jason Calacanis, Natalie and Joe Power, Lars Janowski, Matt Barrie, Michelle Duval, Kellie and Phil Morle,

Shannon Brayton, Timothy Brewer, Jeanmarie and Ray Labonte, Katherine Lancman, Toby Eggleston, Yasmin Grigaliunas, Alan Jones, Anastasia Cammaroto, Angela Manners, Bob Hitching, Caty Germon, Elizabeth Jamae, Georgina Beattie, Karen Kaushansky, Michael Parker, Nick & Petra Dacres-Mannings, Simone James, Karen and Steven Prowse, Tarra Adam, Vicky Clare, Alex De Aboitiz, Alex Germon, Anthony Mansour, Ben Reid, Bob Plankers, Bryan Jackson, Casey Schulz, Cat Mitsunaga, Cate Hull, Clare Hallam, Colleen Blake, Courtney Markgraf, Darren Rogan, David Brown, Emilija Poposka, Erica HooperLee, Gary Culmer, Greg Denehy, Hamish Hawthorn, Holly Cardew, HUMM Corporation, Jaime Fitzgibbon, Jon Fyfe, Kate Kirwin, Klaudia and Ryan Liubinskas, Marcus Schappi, Mikell Taylor, Millie Zinner, Natalie Yan-Chatonsky, Nerida Clare, Nicola Farrell, Paul Millar, Phoebe Adams, Pierre Sauvignon, Rob Antulov, Robett Hollis, Ryan Unmack, Saxon Druce, Silvia Pfeiffer, sunny Goldberg, Terry Hilsberg, Theresa Lim, Tim Bull, Tristan Alexander, Voidan Kardalev, Warwick Anderson, Sally and Wayne Liubinskas, Zoe Alexander, Aileen Guina, Alex Medick, Alice Tiller, Andy Rhodes, Angela del Pino, Ayala Domani, Bryan Luoma, Caroline Lepron, Catherine Hughes, Craig Sisk, Darren Crawford, Diana Barrett, Donna Vyse Hamilton, Drake Taylor, Elane Johnson, Graham Lea, Guy Vincent, Jenny Broderick, John Mabbott, Julie Trell, Katie Nee, Keiji Kanazawa, Leila Pohl, Lizzy Hearne (you were amazing!), Mark Jones, Marshall Taylor, Matt Cameron, Max Antonov, Maxime Girault, Molly Perotti, Natalie Morrone, Nirmal Mehta, Prashan Paramanathan, Rebecca Paget, Ricardo Lopez, Sylvia Bargellini, Terry Parkerpayne, and Tristan Alexander.

Based on the great support (thank you!) I was very lucky to get signed with Mango Publishing. My editor, Natasha, has been a constant source of support, help, and wisdom—thank you so much. To the rest of the Mango team—I was blown away by your teamwork, dedication, and care—you rock!

Extra thanks for to the following people who read through the book at various and multiple points and gave me feedback, ideas and typo fixes: Lizzy Hearne, Caty Germon, Kathey Carreiro, Tim Bull, Sofia Labonte and her book club (as well as Jeanmarie, Ray, Roman and Siena Labonte for being the best neighbors in the world), Karen Kaushansky, Erica Lee, Pippa Galway, Mary Kole (Check out her book on writing kid-lit), Kate Kirwin, Erica HooperLee, Angela Manners, Joanna Dale, Alan Jones (the geeky one), Adelaide Kennedy, Bethany Rawle, and Penelope Brewer. I'm sure I've forgotten someone and I'm so sorry. Please reach out and I'll make it up to you.

And lastly to all the amazing women in the world of science, technology, engineering and mathematics who are building, creating and leading the way—thank you!

About the Author

Mick Liubinskas is a loving dad of two girls and a boy and married to a wonderfully supportive (and patient) woman. He is a high-energy, technology entrepreneur, investor, author, speaker, and industry leader.

He is a big believer that the world will be a happier, better place when we have fairness across gender, race, and culture. He has interviewed more than fifty women in robotics, technology, science, engineering, and math to share their stories and inspire young girls.

Mick is passionate about what individuals can do day in day out to get the planet to sustainability and avoid catastrophic climate change. He doesn't like take-away coffee cups. He programmed his Commodore 64 at age eight, sold computer networks at age seventeen, raised capital at twenty-two, and ran marketing globally for Kazaa at twenty-six.

He has co-founded four technology startup companies, and spent three years in San Francisco. This has included evaluating thousands of ideas, building first products, getting first customers, launching globally, raising capital, closing businesses, selling businesses, and all the emotional rollercoaster rides in between.

Mick is known as Mr. Focus due to his strong drive for starting small and fast, doing fast testing on the road to success and avoiding the entrepreneurial distractions. He co-authored a workbook called Startup Focus which sold five thousand copies.

For fun, he loves surfing, playing football (the round ball variety), and singing bad karaoke. To learn more, visit him online at www.shesbuildingarobot.com.